THE FRIGHTENED MAN

Samuel Coyne sends his ward Diana to enlist detective Paul Rivington as a bodyguard because three attempts have been made on his life. Although he denies knowing the attacker's motive or identity, he has erected elaborate defences around his house. Paul arranges for his brother and partner Bob to take on the job. Later, Bob captures an intruder on the grounds, who recognises Coyne as somebody he calls Kilroe. Surprisingly, Coyne lets the man go, not wishing to prosecute. Then they discover that Diana has mysteriously disappeared . . .

GERALD VERNER

THE FRIGHTENED MAN

Complete and Unabridged

LINFORD
Leicester

First published in Great Britain

First Linford Edition
published 2018

*A catalogue record for this book is available
from the British Library.*

ISBN 978–1–4448–3950–0

Published by
F. A. Thorpe (Publishing)
Anstey, Leicestershire

Set by Words & Graphics Ltd.
Anstey, Leicestershire
Printed and bound in Great Britain by
T. J. International Ltd., Padstow, Cornwall

This book is printed on acid-free paper

1

The Man Who Was Afraid

True to tradition, March, having begun quietly and shyly in a very lamb-like manner, ended with a boisterous demonstration that resulted in serious injury to life and property and helped to fill the newspapers for many days. The winds that swept the country were of gale force, and from all parts of the coast came reports of shipping disasters and damage to sea-fronts and piers. Heavy seas washed away pavilions and shelters and pounded relentlessly at the towering cliffs until in many places great masses crumbled and were engulfed in the boiling surf.

Nor was the havoc any less inland. In the country, trees were uprooted, farm buildings demolished, and chimney stacks blown down by the fury of the tempest. Train services were disorganised everywhere, and many people lost their lives by falling debris.

The storm was at its worst in the north, but the Midlands suffered nearly as badly, and even London and the south did not escape the destructive gale. Hoardings in the suburbs were wrecked, and scaffolding round a block of flats in the course of construction in the West End was reduced to a scattered heap of planking and broken supports. The lorry proceeding along the Portsmouth Road from Southampton was overturned, the driver killed instantly and his mate so badly injured that he died on the way to the hospital.

For four days the hurricane raged, leaving a trail of death and destruction in its wake. And then, during the night of the fifth day, it subsided as suddenly as it had arisen.

Mr. Paul Rivington, coming down to breakfast, found the sun shining and the weather normal once more. Few people would have believed that this tall grey-eyed man had once walked a beat as a uniformed policeman, and yet it was true. At the time of his resignation from the force, he had held the position of an acting inspector in the C.I.D. The commissioner himself had tried to make him reconsider his resignation, but Paul Rivington had pointed out that he had only entered the force in order to acquire a working knowledge of police methods. It was unfair, he argued, since he had a private income in his own right of six thousand a year, that he should stand in the way of the promotion of others. The commissioner was sorry to lose him, and said so; and later Paul found himself in the unique position of being one of the few private detectives whose services were often requisitioned by the Yard when that organisation found itself up against a case in which his special talent might be useful.

He had no office, but conducted his business from the big house overlooking Hampstead Heath which he had inherited, and in which he and his brother Bob had been born. Luckily the advent of the gale had coincided with a more or less slack period, and he had been able to remain indoors clearing up such items of routine work as had accumulated from lack of time to attend to them. Therefore, except on those occasions when he had forced himself to take a short walk for the sake of exercise, he had suffered little inconvenience from the inclement weather.

'The wind seems to have blown itself out,' he remarked as he sat down at the table opposite his brother and poured himself out a cup of coffee.

'A good thing, too,' mumbled Bob with difficulty, his mouth full of eggs and bacon. 'It's done an appalling amount of damage.'

'I'm afraid it has,' agreed Paul, lifting the cover and inspecting the dish in front of him. 'So, for the matter of that, have you — to these eggs and bacon.'

Bob grinned. Fifteen years his brother's junior, he was as unlike him as it was possible for two men to be. Whereas Paul was lean and grey-haired with a slither of moustache lying on his upper lip, Bob was stout and round-faced, with a merry twinkle in his eye and an almost perpetual twitch to the corners of his mouth.

'Sorry,' he mumbled. 'I'll ring for some more.' He half-rose from his chair, but Paul stopped him with a gesture.

'No, there's enough here,' he said. 'I'll make up with toast and marmalade.'

He helped himself to the one rasher and egg that remained and, opening the newspaper that lay folded beside his plate, propped it up against the coffee-pot and began to eat his breakfast in silence.

'What about coming for a walk?' suggested Bob when the meal was over. 'I feel that I can do with a tramp over the Heath after being cooped up here for four days. There's nothing very urgent this morning, is there?'

'You go along,' said his brother, lighting a cigarette. 'I won't come now; I've got one or two letters to write.'

The younger man departed, and Paul settled himself at his desk to deal with his mail. This was usually brought up to him with his early-morning cup of tea, but today there was nothing either of great urgency or interest — one or two bills, a couple of private letters, and a letter from his brokers in the City regarding some shares comprised the entire post. He drew cheques for the bills, answered the private letters, and rang up his brokers to give them the instructions they'd requested concerning certain shares he held. By the time he had done this, he felt in need of another cigarette, and rising to his feet, was in the act of helping himself from a box on the mantelpiece when there came a tap on the door and the maid entered.

'If you please, sir,' she said, 'there's a lady who'd like to see you. She says it's very important.'

'A lady?' Paul's brows drew together. 'What's her name?'

'Miss Diana Fielding, sir.'

'Miss Diana Fielding.' Paul searched his memory without result. 'Do I know her?'

'She's never been here before, sir.'

He hesitated, then: 'Ask her to come in,' he said, and dropped his unlighted cigarette back in the box.

The maid withdrew, and after a short delay reappeared, ushering the visitor into the comfortable study.

6

The woman who entered was quite young, not more than twenty-two or three, and pretty in a pale washed-out way. She stood nervously near the threshold as the servant closed the door behind her and looked at Paul timidly through a pair of large grey eyes. He noticed that she was rather shabbily dressed. Her coat was old and the fur on the collar cheap and worn. The hat perched on the side of her small fair head had once been red, but weather stains and constant cleaning had reduced it to a nondescript shade of patchy pink. There was a net darn in one of her silk stockings, and the tip of a finger showed through the cotton gloves that covered her hands.

'Good morning,' he said, pushing forward a chair. 'Won't you sit down, Miss Fielding, and tell me what I can do for you?'

'Thank you,' she said in a low voice, and coming forward sank into the chair he had offered. 'I've really come to see you, Mr. Rivington, on behalf of my guardian. He's unable to come himself on account of illness, so he sent me.' The well-modulated voice was sweet, with a slight trace of huskiness that added to its charm.

'How can I be of assistance to your guardian?' he asked, sitting down in the chair at his desk and swinging round so that he faced his visitor.

'He wants to see you,' she replied. 'Unfortunately he suffers very badly from rheumatism — so badly at times that he's quite unable to walk. For some days past now it has been worse than usual; and as it's quite impossible for him to leave the house, he asked me to come and see you and try and persuade you to come back with me.'

'You live with your guardian?' he enquired, and she nodded.

'Yes, at Datchet. Our house is called The Wilderness, and is on the edge of the Common. I don't know whether you know the neighbourhood — '

'I know it quite well,' broke in Paul. 'So your guardian wishes to see me. Have you any idea why?'

She shook her head, but there was

uneasiness in her eyes, and a face of fear. 'No,' she answered hesitantly. 'But I think his reason is a very urgent one. In fact I know it is. He told me to tell you it was a matter of life and death.'

Paul was interested. Houses round Datchet Common were large and imposing mansions, the majority of them standing in their own grounds; yet this woman with the lurking fear in her eyes and the lovely voice was wearing clothes that the poorest servant would have despised. 'What's your guardian's name?' he enquired.

'Samuel Coyne.'

He had expected that the name might convey something to him, but he was disappointed. So far as he knew, he had never heard it before.

'I do hope you'll be able to grant his request,' she went on quickly. 'I'm sure there's something very serious behind this. He — he's been so worried lately.'

'What do you mean exactly by 'lately'?' asked Paul as she stopped abruptly. 'When did your guardian first begin to show signs of being worried?'

She seemed reluctant to answer, as though she were afraid of saying more than she ought. 'We first noticed it a month ago,' she answered slowly at length. 'It was just before — just before my guardian had the alarms and trip-wires fixed . . . ' Again she stopped suddenly, her gloved hands plucking nervously at her shabby handbag; and again Paul received the impression that she was fearful of saying more than she should.

'Trip wires and alarms?' he repeated. 'Do you mean Mr. Coyne has recently had burglar alarms fixed to the house?'

'Yes,' she said with a nod. 'And the grounds are wired at night. The servants have instructions to fix them before going to bed. I — I don't know whether I ought to have told you that, Mr. Rivington.'

'Why not?'

'Well, you see — ' She was still playing with the bag on her lap, her eyes averted. ' — Mr. Coyne is rather — well, rather peculiar about some things. He — he might be angry if he thought I'd told you more than I'm supposed to.'

'I see.' Paul nodded, privately deciding that Mr. Samuel Coyne must be something of a martinet. No doubt this accounted for his ward's nervous demeanour; possibly that was the cause of the fear that lurked in her eyes. 'From what you've told me, Miss Fielding,' he went on, 'it seems obvious that your guardian is afraid of something or someone.'

'Yes.' She looked up at him quickly. 'Yes, I — I think he is.'

'Have you any idea of what or whom?'

'No, I know nothing,' she answered hurriedly. 'Nothing at all. Most likely my guardian will tell you himself. Of course he will, or he wouldn't want to see you. You'll come back with me, won't you?'

She looked at him anxiously, and he wondered if her anxiety was entirely on behalf of her guardian. It struck him that it was more personal. She herself was eager for him to accompany her back to Datchet.

'I came in the car,' she continued as he hesitated. 'It's at the door now. We can be home in under two hours. Please say you'll come, Mr. Rivington.'

He looked at the eager face, the scared eyes, and made up his mind. 'Yes, I'll come, Miss Fielding. If you'll wait while I scribble a note to my brother to say where I've gone, I'll be ready to accompany you.'

'Oh, thank you so much!' she breathed gratefully; and for the moment in her relief, the frightened look left her.

He wrote a brief note to Bob explaining the situation, put on his overcoat, and picking up his hat escorted Diana to the door. A shabby little two-seater coupé was drawn up at the side walk, an old-fashioned model of a cheap make of car. Diana took her place at the wheel and Paul climbed into the seat beside her.

During the journey, he put one or two questions to her in the hope of eliciting further information concerning the household to which he was going, but she was very reticent in her replies. It was evident that having carried out her instructions and persuaded him to return with her, she was fearful of overstepping her authority.

The little car might be old, but it ran

well. It was barely two hours after leaving Hampstead that they came in sight of the house. It was an ugly building of stone, square and squat, and it stood amid a forest of trees. A high wall surrounded it, broken only so far as Paul could see by the heavy gates that gave admittance to the short drive. These were high and solid and apparently locked; for, bringing the car to a halt, Diana got down with a little apology and tugged at a wrought-iron bell-pull.

She had to wait some time before there was any answer, and then a grille was opened and Paul caught the vague glimpse of a man's face staring through. The grille closed, there was the rasp of a key, and the gates opened. Diana came back to the car and drove it through the entrance, and immediately the gates were swung to and relocked. Paul pursed his lips. An unusual proceeding. Samuel Coyne's fear must be very great indeed if, even in broad daylight, he took this precaution to keep people out.

The car stopped again beside a pillared porch. 'Will you come in, Mr. Rivington?'

Diana said, getting out. He nodded and followed her up a flight of steps into a gloomy hall sparsely furnished in old-fashioned oak. The polished floor was bare of carpets, but a couple of rugs helped a little to take off the austereness which was a predominant feature of the place. A shadow loomed in the open doorway behind them, and the man who had blocked the gates came in.

Paul had only caught a vague glimpse of him before; but now that he could see him more clearly, he was not impressed. He was a burly fellow of large build with an unpleasant face. He gave Paul a sharp glance as he crossed the hall but said nothing, disappearing through a door that apparently led to the back portion of the house.

'If you'll come in here,' Diana said, ushering the detective into a long room that was furnished as a lounge, 'I'll tell my guardian we've arrived.'

She left him, closing the door behind her, and he strolled over to a big window that gave on to the garden. The view was not prepossessing. The lozenge-shaped

14

lawn was rank and had seen neither shears nor mower for a considerable time. No attempt had been made to cultivate the weed-grown beds or trim the shrubbery. A broken-down pergola covered the long path that stretched away to the dimness of a mass of trees. A gloomy and desolate place. It was not surprising, he thought, that Diana was subdued. Living in these surroundings was sufficient to depress anyone.

He was full of curiosity to know *why* Samuel Coyne wished to see him, and to learn the reason for the locked gates and alarms and trip-wires Diana had mentioned. Of what was this man afraid? He turned from his contemplation of the neglected garden as the door opened and she came back.

'My guardian will see you in his study,' she said, 'just across the hall.'

She led the way to a door almost facing that of the lounge, and Paul entered a small dingy apartment in which there were many books. A man seated in a wheelchair in front of a large flat-topped desk looked up.

'It was good of you to come, Mr. Rivington,' he said. 'And I must apologise for having put you to so much trouble. Please sit down.'

Paul took the chair indicated, taking stock of the man before him. He had expected an old man, and was a little surprised to discover that Samuel Coyne could scarcely be more than forty-five or fifty. His rather swarthy face was thin and lined and his hair was black and thick, without a tinge of grey. The hands that gripped the arms of the invalid chair looked strong and capable.

'Why did you wish to see me, Mr. Coyne?' he asked.

The other did not answer at once, and Paul got the impression that he was choosing his words carefully.

'I wished to see you,' he said at length, 'because I believe myself to be in very great danger.'

Paul raised his eyebrows. 'Of what?'

'Of being murdered!' was the reply.

2

The Menace of the Unknown

'I presume,' said Paul, after waiting for Coyne to add something to his surprising statement, 'that you have a very good reason for this belief?'

'A very good reason,' the other said with a nod. 'Otherwise I should not have wasted your time.' He leaned forward, flicked open a box in front of him, helped himself to a cigarette, and lit it. 'A very good reason indeed, Mr. Rivington,' he continued. 'Three attempts have already been made on my life.'

'Indeed!' Paul was a little startled at this assertion. 'When did these attempts of which you speak take place?'

'The first occurred a month ago,' replied Coyne, speaking slowly and deliberately, and again giving him the impression that he was weighing every word before it was uttered. 'I'd been over to dinner with a neighbour of mine. It was a fine night, and when I'm free from these attacks that occasionally cripple me I'm fond of exercise, and I walked home. The way is rather a lonely one and cuts across the Common. As I say, the night was fine and there was a moon. I left my friend's house at a little after ten, and I'd just reached a small clump of trees that skirt the footpath a hundred yards or so from my own place when somebody fired from the darkness, and my hat was shot from my head. A second bullet passed through my coat sleeve. I didn't wait for a third; I took to my heels and ran the remaining distance that separated me from home.'

He paused and moistened his lips, and Paul remained silent, waiting for him to continue. 'The second attempt occurred the day before yesterday,' he went on. 'I'm not a very good sleeper, and it's usually long after the rest of my household have gone to bed that I myself retire. I usually sit up working or reading until two, sometimes three, in the morning. On the night I'm speaking of, it was nearly two before I decided to go to bed. The gale was at its height and the noise it was making was terrific. I hadn't been out for three days, and in spite of the storm I decided that I should like a breath of air before going up to my room. My servant had, of course, locked up, but I unchained and unbolted the front door and stood on the steps for a moment or two looking out into the darkness of the garden. It was more or less sheltered in the porch, and I was in the act of turning to re-enter the house, when something swished past my head and struck the door behind me with a thud. It was a knife! Had I not moved when I did, it would have buried itself in my throat instead of the panel of the door.'

His voice shook at the recollection, and Paul saw his forehead go moist with perspiration. 'You saw no one on either occasion?' he asked.

'No,' Coyne replied. 'I saw no one. The shots were fired from the clump of trees I mentioned. The knife came, as far as I can make out, from a belt of shrubbery near the drive.'

'You have the knife?' Paul asked.

For answer Coyne stretched out a hand, pulled open a drawer in his desk, and took out a long thin-bladed knife, which he passed across to his visitor. It was razor-sharp and possessed a weighty handle. The detective examined it, holding it by the blade, although the precaution occurred to him as rather belated since any fingerprints there might have been had probably been obliterated by Coyne when had removed it from the door panel. He mentioned this to the man.

'I'm afraid it never occurred to me,' Coyne confessed. 'In my agitation I never thought of handling the thing carefully.'

Paul laid the weapon down on the desk. 'And the third attempt?' he said.

'The third attempt occurred yesterday,' answered the other gravely. 'The wind dropped a little during the evening; and although the night had brought on a more than usually severe attack of rheumatism, which made it impossible for me to walk, I wheeled myself out in this chair into the garden. I was propelling myself along the path that runs near the boundary wall when there was a sharp report, and a bullet came within an inch of my head. I didn't stop to investigate, but as I hurried back to the house I thought I heard the sound of somebody scrambling over the wall.'

Paul surveyed him steadily, his interest rapidly growing. It had occurred to him at first that possibly the frightened Mr. Coyne was suffering from hallucinations. He had interviewed many people who had been under the impression that their lives were in danger without any tangible cause for this belief. It was one of the most common forms of mania, and Paul had met it many times. During the man's recital, he had searched for signs that might confirm this first impression, but he had failed to find them. He was forced to the conclusion that the man before him was speaking the truth. That he was desperately afraid was evident — it was visible in every movement; visible most in the deep-set, shifting eyes.

'You've notified the police, of course?' he remarked, and to his surprise Samuel

Coyne shook his head.

'No, I haven't. I have no wish to bring the police into this matter. That's why I've consulted you.'

'But why? Surely the police would be the best people for you to go to?'

'I don't wish the matter to become public property,' answered the other curtly.

It was not a very convincing reason, and Paul was not at all sure that it was the true one, but he let it pass. 'Have you any idea why these attempts should have been made on your life?' he asked.

'No,' Coyne replied slowly after a pause. 'I have no idea at all.'

'Then why,' said Rivington, 'do you anticipate a fourth?'

'The person responsible has tried three times and failed, so it seems only natural to me that he'll try again.'

There was a certain amount of common sense in this reasoning, but Paul was convinced that the man was keeping a lot back. There was something very peculiar about the whole affair. A normal person would have immediately notified the police unless he had some very good reason for not doing so, and the reason which Coyne had given was not a good one. He was not at all impressed either by the man's manner or his appearance. The fear that filled him was greater than the circumstances seemed to warrant. It was the terror of the known, not of the unknown. His denial of any knowledge concerning the reason for these attacks on him was a lie. He knew very well what lay behind these attempts on his life, and it was this knowledge that had instilled in him the fear of death which showed in his small eyes.

'It seems to me, Mr. Coyne,' he said after a long pause, 'that I can do very little to help you. The best advice I can offer you is to lay the whole matter before the police and ask for their protection.'

'I can't do that!' said Samuel Coyne, and his mouth set stubbornly.

Paul's shoulders went up in an almost imperceptible shrug. 'What was your idea when you sent for me?'

'I hoped,' said the other quickly, 'that you would investigate this business. It was my intention to suggest that you should stay here for a few days and try to discover who is responsible for — for this persecution.'

'I fail to see what good that would do,' answered Rivington, shaking his head. 'There's nothing to suggest that this fourth attempt you fear, even if it's made at all, will occur within the next few days, and it would be impossible for me to prolong my stay indefinitely. I'm afraid I can only repeat my suggestion that you should consult the police.'

'Does that mean,' said Mr. Coyne, and his voice was not quite steady, 'that you refuse to help me?'

'I'm afraid I can't. What you require is a bodyguard, Mr. Coyne, and I'm not prepared to act in that capacity.'

'Is there nothing I can do that will make you change your mind?' asked the man tremulously. 'I'm prepared to agree to anything, within reason, if you'll accede to my wishes.'

'There's only one thing that might make me change my mind,' said Paul, stressing the *might*, 'and I'm going to speak candidly. If you tell me the whole truth concerning this matter, then there is a possibility that I might see my way to helping you. That's as far as I'm prepared to go.'

The swarthy face flushed with anger. 'I don't know what you mean!' Coyne's voice was harsh. 'I've told you all I know, Mr. Rivington. I can't tell you any more than I have. I don't usually beg favours of anyone, but I entreat you to reconsider your decision. I will pay any fee you like to name — ' He broke off as the door was opened without ceremony and the surly-faced man who had opened the gates came in.

'Telegram just come fer you,' he grunted ungraciously, and flung the orange envelope in front of his employer.

'For me?' Coyne's voice was surprised. He stared at the wire on his blotting pad and then, snatching it up, tore it open.

Paul saw the colour recede from his face as he read the message.

'Read that!' he said thickly. 'Read it!'

Paul took the oblong slip of paper from his trembling fingers and read the scrawled lines in pencilled writing. The telegram had been handed in at Datchet Post Office and was addressed to

'*Coyne. The Wilderness.*'

It ran:

'*Rivington can't save you. No one can.*'

There was no signature.

Paul looked at the timing. It had been handed in half an hour previously.

3

'You see?' croaked Coyne hoarsely, as Paul laid the flimsy slip down on the desk. 'The fact that I've communicated with you is known, that's why that was sent.'

'Known to whom?' asked the detective.

'To the person responsible for these attacks on me,' answered the man in the wheelchair.

'Are you suggesting that Miss Fielding was followed this morning when she came to call on me?'

'What other explanation can there be? That telegram obviously refers to your presence here. It mentions you by name. What other explanation can there be?' He swung round quickly, suddenly becoming aware that the unpleasant-faced servant was listening curiously. 'You can go, Gunter,' he said.

The man hesitated, and then, shrugging his shoulders, crossed reluctantly to the door and went out. There was a silence after he had gone, broken at last by Coyne. 'You still refuse to help me, Mr. Rivington?' he asked.

Paul frowned. 'I can only repeat my former advice, which is that you should lay the whole matter before the police.'

'And nothing will induce you to change your mind?' asked Coyne.

Paul shook his head. 'I can't, of course, force you to act for me,' Coyne said. 'But I regret very deeply your attitude. I've already told you the reason why I don't wish to consult the police on this matter, and although I realise that from your point of view it seems the most sensible thing to do, it's impossible. If you won't undertake what I ask, then I must prepare to face this unknown danger by myself and risk the consequences.'

'Are you sure,' said Paul, eyeing him steadily, 'that it's so entirely unknown to you?'

Samuel Coyne's thin face hardened. 'That's the second time, Mr. Rivington,' he said stiffly, 'that you've suggested I'm lying. What exactly do you mean?'

'I mean, is there nothing that can suggest to you the reason for these attempts on your life or the identity of the person responsible for them?'

'Nothing! I've assured you, Mr. Rivington, that I'm completely ignorant of the source from which this danger emanates. That's what makes it all the more — frightening.' He paused and moistened his lips with the tip of his tongue. 'If I knew who was responsible, and the reason, I should find it easier to deal with. It's this groping in the dark, this living in the shadow of a menace, the very nature of which I have no knowledge, that's so frightening. I *admit* I'm frightened. It would be useless denying it.'

The words were uttered with a disarming frankness, but there was no ring of truth behind them. The man was lying, and the knowledge of this counteracted any effect the appeal might have had. At the same time, Paul was forced to admit that he was interested. What really lay behind this man's fear? An idea suggested itself to him and he put it into words.

'Perhaps, Mr. Coyne,' he said, 'I may be able to help you, though not in the way you originally had in mind. It's quite impossible for me to spare sufficient time to act in the capacity of bodyguard; but if it'll satisfy you, I'll send my brother to look into the matter. He can, if you wish, take up his residence here, and you can rely on him as much as if you were dealing with me.'

Coyne's eyes lighted. 'I accept your offer, Mr. Rivington,' he said without hesitation, and there was relief in his voice. 'I accept your offer, and I'm exceedingly grateful.'

'I have one stipulation to make, however. If this business should develop into a matter for the police, my brother must be allowed to call them in at his own discretion.'

The other's face clouded, and the detective thought he was going to refuse; but after an interval, he nodded reluctantly. 'Very well,' he acceded. 'When can I expect your brother to arrive?'

'I'll send him down at six o'clock this evening.'

'A room shall be prepared for him, and I'll do everything to make him comfortable.' Coyne stretched out his hand as he finished speaking and pressed a bell on his desk. 'You don't know,' he went on, 'what a relief this will be for me. My affliction practically renders me helpless, and therefore at the mercy of this unknown person who seeks my life. The presence of your brother will be a great comfort — ' He broke off and looked up as the surly-faced servant entered. 'Gunter,' he said, 'tell Annie a friend of mine is coming down this evening to stay for a few days. See that she gets the room next to mine ready.'

'All right, I'll tell her,' growled Gunter.

'And,' continued his employer, 'send Miss Fielding to me.'

'She's out,' grunted the servant.

'Out?' Coyne frowned. 'Where's she gone?'

'How should I know?' snarled Gunter. 'I ain't 'er keeper, am I?'

'There's no need to be impudent!' snapped Coyne. 'Did she say how long she'd be?'

'She didn't say nothing,' was the sullen reply.

Coyne pursed his lips. There was an angry light in his eyes and two spots of red appeared on his cheeks. 'Tell her I want her as soon as she comes in!' he snapped, and Gunter departed. 'Will you stay to lunch, Mr. Rivington?' he asked, and Paul saw that he was making a desperate effort to control his temper.

'No, thank you,' Paul said. 'I must be getting back.'

'If you wait for a minute or two, Diana — my ward — will drive you back. She can't be very long. She had no right to go out without letting me know.'

'I wouldn't dream of troubling Miss Fielding,' said Paul quickly. 'I can quite easily go back by train.'

'She should be here, all the same,' grunted Coyne angrily. 'She had no right to go off like this without saying where she was going.'

Paul thought he was making a lot of fuss about nothing, but he kept this thought to himself. Taking his leave of the scowling Mr. Coyne, he was escorted to the gate by the equally ill-tempered Gunter. The impulse that had prompted him to make the suggestion regarding Bob was one of curiosity, and already he was beginning to regret it. There was something about the atmosphere of The Wilderness that grated. In spite of its owner's efforts to be pleasant, Paul had taken a dislike to him. It was peculiar, too, the way in which the servant Gunter addressed his master, and more peculiar than a man like Coyne should suffer such open rudeness so mildly. He was not the type of man to tolerate insolence from an employee, and yet both Gunter's manner and speech had been openly so. Altogether a queer household, thought Paul as he walked across the common towards Datchet. And not the least queer was Diana. Was that scared look in her eyes the result of knowledge concerning the danger that threatened her guardian, or was it due to something else?

He was still thinking about her when he saw her standing by the gate of a small house on the other side of the common. She was talking to a lean brown-faced man, and was so engrossed in her conversation that she failed to notice Paul as he passed. So that was where she had gone, he thought, and smiled. It was not unnatural. She was a pretty woman, and there could be little to attract her in the gloomy atmosphere of the house he had just left.

He wondered idly whether Mr. Coyne was aware of this obvious friendship between his ward and the good-looking neighbour. Possibly he was not; more than possibly he would have resented it. It was evident that Diana Fielding's life was scarcely her own; that this man with the sallow face and frightened eyes ruled her with the iron hand of a despot.

He came out by the river, walked along past the boat-house with its array of craft that gives to Datchet almost the air of a seaside town, and turning to the right made his way to the station. He was passing the post office when an idea occurred to him, and he went in.

'I want,' he said pleasantly to the assistant behind the counter, 'some information.'

She looked at him enquiringly.

'About an hour and a half ago,' continued Paul, 'a telegram was handed in here for Mr. Coyne of The Wilderness. Remember it?'

The woman nodded. 'Yes, sir. I thought it was rather peculiar. We don't usually get a telegram handed in here for delivery in the district.'

'No, naturally,' agreed Rivington. 'It means of course, that you merely make a copy of it and send it out by the boy?'

'That's right, sir,' said the woman, 'and in this case I can't see why Miss Fielding couldn't have given the message to Mr. Coyne herself.'

'Miss Fielding?' repeated Paul, and the surprise in his voice was genuine.

The woman nodded. 'Yes, sir. It was Miss Fielding who handed in the telegram.'

He left the post office after murmuring a vague excuse for his enquiry, completely mystified. The telegram that had so apparently upset its recipient had been handed in by Diana Fielding. Did that mean she was working in collusion with the unknown person responsible for the attempts on her guardian's life? Was this the reason for her reticence and her fear when she had called on him? It was certainly a sufficient explanation, and yet she had been genuinely anxious for him to accede to Coyne's request, and he was pretty certain that that anxiety hadn't been entirely on that frightened man's behalf. She had wanted him to come for her own sake. But surely, if she was in the plot against her guardian, the last thing she would have wished was Paul's interference?

It was extraordinary, and though he tried to puzzle it out on the journey back to London, he found no satisfactory solution.

Bob was in when he reached the Hampstead house, and listened with interest to what his brother had to tell him. 'It sounds as if it might lead to something exciting,' he remarked — and just how prophetic his words were, they were both to realise before many days had passed.

At half-past four, he left with instructions from Paul to notify him should any developments occur. When they did, however, he was far too busy to pay much attention, for he had become involved in a crime the aspects of which seemed remote from the affairs of the frightened Mr. Coyne of Datchet; although, as was afterwards proved, there was the closest of links between them.

4

The Man with the Shaven Head

It was long past midnight, and the respectable inhabitants of Hampstead were warmly in bed and asleep. Spaniards Road, which ran along by the edge of the heath and beyond down a steep incline through Highgate village and so into the open country, was deserted.

All the evening a drizzle of rain had been falling, and the shiny pavements reflected blearily the economically spaced street lamps that bordered them. It was a chill, unpleasant night with a keen wind that blew fitfully, stirring the trees and bushes in the waste ground at the side of the dismal stretch of road, so that they kept up a continuous agitated whisper as though aware of what was to happen in their vicinity.

A clock somewhere struck one. The passing vibration of the bell blended with the faint hum of a high-powered engine, and presently from the direction of Highgate a large saloon car came into view, its brilliant headlights illuminating the road for a considerable distance and turning the puddles into splashes of shimmering light. It was travelling at high speed, but as it crested the hill that led onto this almost straight stretch of road through to Hampstead it slowed, and halfway along drew into the side and came to a halt.

The driver, a muffled figure in a huge overcoat and wearing a pair of mica goggles, switched off the headlights, and opening the door, got down from the driving seat onto the pavement. Pausing by the side of the stationary car, he listened and scanned the desolate thoroughfare quickly to the right and left. There was a certain furtiveness in his actions that lent a sinister air to the proceedings and gave the impression that he was engaged in some illegal act. The silence was unbroken save for the irregular dripping of the rain from the trees and bushes nearby.

It was a melancholy spot, scarcely the place one would choose to linger in; but apparently the man in the big coat thought otherwise, for having assured himself that he was the only living thing in sight, and that the road was quite deserted, he hurriedly opened the back door of the saloon, and leaning half through, felt about on the floor of the dark interior. Quickly, almost with feverish haste, he began to pull a heavy object out onto the wet pavement: a grim thing that hung limp and lifeless in his arms as he moved it to the edge of the path so that it lay half over the grassy slope of the waste land.

He was breathing heavily, and beneath the goggles his face was dewed with perspiration. Suddenly he straightened up as a sound came to his ears in the short lull following a heavy gust of wind — the faint sound of measured footfalls from somewhere down the dark stretch of road. It was scarcely audible, and as the wind rose again it was drowned by the rustling of the leaves; but it was sufficient to send a wave of panic through the man who heard it.

Running quickly back to the car, he hastily climbed into the seat behind the wheel. At a touch of his foot, the engine sprang into life and the big machine moved forward, gathering speed quickly as the driver pressed hard on the accelerator. It passed Police Constable Finlay as he rounded the bend at the end of Spaniards Road, but he only glanced casually at it, and it had faded from his mind almost before the noise of the engine had vanished in the distance. Later he was to remember it, and curse himself for having failed to notice the number.

Finlay was a young man, and hadn't long been a member of the police force. But during that short time, he had exhibited signs of intelligence that had caused him to be marked for promotion at the first opportunity. His thoughts were not unpleasant ones in spite of the discomfort caused by the coldness of the night and the knowledge of the dreary hours that lay in front of him before he was relieved. His inspector had that day offered a word of praise concerning his handling of a small enquiry connected with a shop theft, and in consequence his mind was full of plans for the future as he paced along his beat with that measured tread that is peculiar to members of the constabulary. His way took him past the spot where, a few moments before, the saloon had waited.

As he approached the place, a gust of wind caught the end of his waterproof cape and tore it open. The wind was strong and the force of the impact caused him to stagger slightly, and brought him nearer to the unprotected edge of the path, where it joined the grassy slope beyond. He shivered in spite of his heavy clothing as he drew his cape closer around him, and at the same instant his foot struck something and he stumbled. He recovered his balance, and loosening the electric lamp from his belt switched it on, throwing the light on the ground at his feet.

The 'feel' of the something that had nearly tripped him up had brought his heart to his mouth and, as he saw what the white beam revealed, he knew that he hadn't been mistaken. Lying half on the path, and half on the grassy bank at one side, was the huddled figure of a man, face downwards!

Finlay's breath whistled through his teeth as he stopped and turned the limp form on its back. A glance told him that the man was dead — and then he saw something that almost caused him to drop his lamp, so unexpected and horrible was the spectacle.

The man was dressed shabbily in ragged patched trousers of some dark material. He wore no waistcoat or collar, and the shirt revealed by the half-open coat was grimy and torn at the neck. But it was none of these things which brought astonishment to the rather prominent eyes of the policeman. It was the man's head, hairless and shining in the light of the lantern, and scarred with innumerable tiny cuts; a head that was completely bald, and not naturally bald but bald because the hair had been shaved from the skull with a razor.

'My God!' muttered Finlay; and the

hand that sought his whistle shook a little, for there was something beastly and obscene about that unnaturally hairless head.

The shrill screech of the whistle split the stillness of the night coincidently with the lights of a car coming into view at the end of the road.

Paul Rivington, driving home from a visit to some friends, heard it and the faint answering call that came from some distance away. Staring through the rain-spattered glass of the windscreen, he saw the headlights of the car glisten on the policeman's wet cape by the side of the road, and, slowing, came to a halt beside the burly figure.

'What's the trouble, Officer?' he asked, leaning out.

At the sound of his voice, the man turned and directed the light of the lantern on his face. 'Oh, it's you, Mr. Rivington!' he exclaimed in surprise. 'I thought I recognised your voice when you spoke.'

'I heard you whistle and wondered if I could be of any assistance. What's happened, Finlay?' He had met the young policeman several times, and had been one of the first to bring his smartness to the notice of the higher officials at Scotland Yard.

'It's a queer affair, sir,' answered Finlay. 'It's murder, I think — ' He broke off as the sound of heavy running footfalls came from along the road. 'This'll be the sergeant, I expect,' he muttered. Paul got out of the car as a sergeant and another constable came up at a run.

'What's up, Finlay?' panted the sergeant, a stout heavily built man. 'An accident?'

'No, sir. It's murder, I think,' replied Finlay. 'This is Mr. Rivington, who was near and heard my whistle.'

'How d'you do, Mr. Rivington,' said the sergeant, touching his helmet. 'You'll remember me, Sergeant Bolter. I worked with you on the Fernlea robbery.'

Paul nodded. 'I remember you quite well, Sergeant.'

Bolter turned to Finlay. 'Murder, did you say?' he enquired sharply.

'Yes, sir,' answered the constable. He

pointed, and Bolter moved over to the still form and bent down. They heard his breath hiss sharply as he confirmed Finlay's statement.

'Queer,' he muttered. 'His head's been shaved, and recently. What do you make of it, Mr. Rivington?'

Paul crossed over to the body and stopped. The face was that of a middle-aged man with flabby unhealthy cheeks and a thick-lipped mouth, and there was no doubt concerning the sergeant's assertion. Every vestige of hair had been removed from the skull, and by a none-too-skilful person, as the many razor cuts testified. Paul experienced a quickened interest. The shaven head lifted this crime from the ordinary rut and stimulated his imagination.

The dead man appeared to have been of excellent physique. A shabby cloth hat lay a foot from his head and was in keeping with the rest of his clothing, but neither tallied with the well-fed body and smooth skin.

'Have you searched him?' asked Paul, looking up at Finlay.

'No, sir,' answered the policeman. 'There wasn't time. I blew my whistle at once.'

'How did he come by his death?' put in Sergeant Bolter.

Paul gently turned the limp form over and pointed silently to an ominous stain on the ragged jacket between the shoulder blades. 'Stabbed!' he answered briefly, and there could be no doubt as to the truth of his words. The back of the jacket was caked with blood and the cloth had been cut, a long narrow slit where the knife had entered.

The sergeant leaned forward and touched the blood marks lightly with his fingertips. 'Looks as if he's been dead some considerable time,' he muttered. 'This blood has dried hard.'

'It also seems to indicate that he wasn't killed here,' said Paul. 'In this damp atmosphere, the blood wouldn't have dried.' He pursed his lips. 'I suppose we'd better search the poor fellow's pockets and see if there's anything to establish his identity.'

The sergeant agreed, and they made a

rapid search, but without result. The pockets were empty. Neither did a hurried examination reveal any marks on his clothing. There was nothing at all to show the dead's man's identity.

The sergeant turned to the constable who had accompanied him to the scene of the discovery. 'You'd better go and phone the station for an ambulance and the divisional surgeon,' he directed. 'Get on to the inspector and ask him to come up as quickly as possible.'

The man saluted and hurried away, and Paul continued his examination of the dead man. He peered closely at his hands. The nails were manicured and well cared for, and the skin was smooth and of a fine texture. He wrinkled his brows and looked up at the sergeant, who had been watching interestedly. 'Rather a puzzling affair, Bolter,' he murmured.

'Yes, sir,' agreed Bolter. 'I was thinking the same.'

Turning his attention to the naked skull, Paul closely scrutinised it. 'Bring your lamp nearer, Finlay,' he grunted; and when the constable did so: 'It looks to me as if the head was shaved after death. The razor's made quite a considerable gash here but it's scarcely bled at all. If it'd been done while the heart was in action, there would've been a lot more blood.'

The astonished sergeant removed his helmet and scratched his head. 'Why on earth,' he demanded, 'should anyone have wanted to shave him?'

'One reason might be a desire to prevent identification,' suggested Paul, 'though I'll admit it's not a very convincing one. I'm certain he was never killed here — the bloodstains bear that out; and apart from that, his clothes are almost dry.' He rose, moved a little way down the grassy slope, and examined the dead man's shoes. 'There's not a trace of wet or mud upon them!' he announced. 'There would've been, had he stood in this vicinity for even a short period.'

'How d'you think he got here, then?' asked Bolter.

'Brought in a car most likely,' answered Paul. 'That seems the most probable explanation.'

'A large saloon car passed me as I came

by the pond, sir,' put in Finlay. 'It was going at a fair speed and came from this direction.'

The sergeant looked at him quickly. 'Notice the number?' he asked.

'No, sir,' said the constable regretfully. 'There was no necessity to, though of course if I'd suspected there was anything wrong — '

'It's quite possible there was nothing wrong with the car you saw,' interrupted Paul. 'It may not have been concerned in any way with this affair. But the body could not have been here long before you discovered it. Anything else pass you?'

Finlay shook his head. 'No, sir. I came straight up East Hill and stopped for several minutes talking to Hales before he moved off on his beat.'

'So if there'd been any other vehicle, it would have passed you at that point?' said the sergeant.

'Unless,' put in Paul, 'it turned off the side road opposite the pond.'

'Even then I should have seen it, sir,' said Finlay. 'There was nothing in either direction until the saloon passed.'

'It looks as if that saloon is the car we want,' said the sergeant. 'Did you see who was in it?'

'I saw the driver,' replied Finlay. 'The interior of the car was in darkness. You couldn't tell whether there was anyone else in it or not.'

'Could you identify the driver?' asked Paul.

The constable shook his head. 'Afraid I couldn't, sir. He was so muffled up that you couldn't tell whether it was a man or a woman. I'm almost sure it was a man though, because he was wearing goggles. I caught the glint of them as he passed.'

The sergeant sighed disappointedly. 'Next to impossible to trace the car,' he said, 'unless the man on point duty further down the road can give any information. I'll make enquiries when I get back to the station.'

Paul took the lantern from Finlay's hand and threw the beam on the gravel path. At a point near the end of the kerb, he stopped and bent down slightly. 'Something heavy has been dragged over the path just here,' he said; and joining

51

him, the sergeant saw the marks on the wet tarmac that he alluded to. They crossed the pavement at right angles from the direction of the roadway.

Paul's eyes travelled the road itself. Level with the marks on the sidewalk, about four yards in front of his own car, were the impressions of tyres, and between them a spot of black oil. 'A car has recently stopped here,' he said. 'And a large one, by the space between the wheels.'

A bell sounded in the distance, and shortly afterwards the ambulance arrived. With it came the police doctor and an inspector who listened while Bolter gave them the details of the discovery.

'We'll send out a hurry call about the car to all stations at once,' he said when the sergeant had finished. 'There's just a chance somebody might have seen it.' He knelt beside the dead man and confirmed what had already been told him. 'All right, carry on, doctor,' he said briefly. 'We can't shift him until after the photographers have been. They're following on.' He turned to Paul as the doctor took his place. 'I suppose you'll be coming to the station, Mr. Rivington?'

Paul shook his head. 'No, I'll be getting home; there's nothing further I can do. But if you discover any clues to the dead man's identity or anything else concerning this business, you might phone me. I'm rather interested.'

The inspector promised.

'Extraordinary affair,' he said, as Paul got into his car. 'Why the man's head should have been shaved beats me.'

'That's what makes it so interesting,' answered Rivington. 'I'm inclined to think there's something very big behind it.'

How true his words were was to be revealed during the course of the next few days.

5

The Alarm

Bob reached Datchet at a little before six, and as he came out of the station it began to rain. It was only a light shower, and he decided to walk to Mr. Coyne's isolated habitation. Turning up the collar of his mackintosh and gripping his suitcase, he set off.

Paul had given him explicit instructions for finding the place, and he experienced no difficulty. Twenty minutes later, he was surveying the forbidding gates and high wall unenthusiastically. Seen in the fading light of that March day, it looked anything but inviting. The gaunt trees rose blackly against the lowering sky; a tracery of leafless branches, the tiny buds as yet but a promise of the green that would come later. A desolate, depressing house from the outside; a house whose appearance bred distrust.

Bob raised his hand and pulled the bell. He had to wait a long time before he got an answer to his summons, so long that he was wondering if his ring had been heard, and had raised his hand to repeat it when the grille was slammed back and the face of the man who from his brother's description he recognised as Gunter peered through.

'Who is it? What d'you want?' asked the man harshly.

'My name's Rivington,' said Bob a little curtly. 'Mr. Coyne's expecting me.'

The small hard eyes of the man behind the gate peered at him closely; then the lock snapped and one side of the heavy gates was pulled open. 'Come in,' said the servant ungraciously. Bob picked up his bag and crossed the threshold, waiting while the other shut and relocked the gates.

'This way,' growled Gunter when he had completed his task; and without bothering to see if he was being followed or not, he set off up the neglected drive, making no attempt to take the suitcase from Bob's hand. The front door of the house was open, and ascending the steps, they entered the hall.

'Coyne's in his study,' said the broad-shouldered servant. 'I'll tell him you've come.' He led the way over to the door, and without troubling to knock, twisted the handle and opened it. 'Here's your friend,' he said grumpily.

Samuel Coyne, sitting by a meagre fire in his wheelchair, looked round as Bob entered. 'Good evening, Mr. Rivington,' he said. 'Gunter, take that suitcase and put it in the room next to mine.'

The man obeyed sullenly, and when he had gone his employer offered an apology. 'I'm afraid Gunter's rather uncouth,' he said. 'But he's a good servant and it's difficult to get anyone these days.'

Bob, sensing the atmosphere of that gloomy house, was not surprised. Few people, he thought, would be prepared to serve Mr. Coyne under the prisonlike circumstances with which he surrounded himself.

'Would you mind shutting the door?' Coyne went on, for the servant had left it open; and when Bob had complied with his request: 'I presume Mr. Rivington told you the position?'

'Yes,' Bob said, nodding. 'I understand that three attempts have already been made on your life, and you fear a fourth.'

'That's right,' Coyne assented. 'I've taken certain precautions, but in my condition — ' He tapped one arm of the wheelchair with his fingers. ' I can't get about as quickly as I should like. Therefore I feel in need of protection.'

Paul had mentioned the alarms and trip-wires Diana Fielding had told him were fixed at night, and Bob concluded that the 'precautions' referred to by the man before him were these. A question confirmed this supposition.

'Yes,' he said. 'I had them put in after the first attempt. There's an alarm in every room, attached to wires in the grounds. If any unauthorised person succeeds in climbing the walls, a loud tone buzzer rings. I'll get my ward to show you the system after dinner. Now I expect you'd like to see your room. We dine early — seven o'clock. Would you mind touching that bell?'

Bob pressed the button on the desk; and after a short delay there was a tap on the door, and a maid appeared nervously on the threshold.

'Take Mr. Rivington up to the room that has been prepared for him,' ordered Coyne curtly, and Bob followed the woman up a dark staircase to a broad landing. Two passages branched off this, and entering the right hand one, she stopped before the first door on the left and held it open.

'Would you like some hot water, sir?' she asked.

'Please,' said Bob, surveying the cheerless room beyond without enthusiasm.

She hurried away, closing the door behind her, and he looked around him. The bedroom that had been assigned to him was large and barely furnished. A big old-fashioned brass bedstead, a washstand, a chest of drawers and a chair constituted the bulk. The floor was covered with threadbare linoleum on which two old and ragged rugs had been laid, one near the bed and the other in front of the fireplace. Eyeing the apartment disparagingly, Bob devoutly hoped that his stay at The Wilderness would not be a long one.

There was an air of poverty about the whole place that puzzled him. This man, Coyne, had offered Rivington any sum he liked to name to investigate the attempts on his life, and yet the appearance of the house suggested that money was scarce.

His bag had been left at the foot of the bed, and lifting it, he undid the strap and proceeded to unpack the few belongings he had brought with him. This occupied him only a few minutes, and since there was no sign of the maid returning with the water, he strolled over to the window and looked out.

The rain was falling more heavily and dusk was advancing rapidly. In the dim light, he caught a vista of neglected garden enclosed by the gaunt trees which he hadn't noticed on his arrival. A cheerless and uninspiring scene. Opening the window, he leaned out. The smell of decaying vegetation reached his nostrils and he shivered. Anything could happen in this place, he thought, and turned away as the maid came back with his hot water.

She set it down on the washstand and enquired nervously if there was anything else he wanted. When Bob replied in the negative, she departed, and he proceeded, after drawing the curtains and switching on the light, to wash leisurely.

His first meeting with Samuel Coyne hadn't impressed him in the man's favour, and having no wish for another tête-à-tête interview with his host, he dawdled, whiling away the time until his watch told him it was five minutes to seven. He was on the point of leaving the room to go down when he remembered something, and opening his suitcase, took out a small compact automatic. Examining it quickly, he made certain that there was a clip of cartridges in the butt, pulled back the jacket, flipped one into the breech, and pressing home the safety catch stowed the weapon away in his hip pocket. It might not be necessary, but on the other hand the feel of it against his hip was reassuring.

He came out of the room, and

descending the stairs saw a woman crossing the hall. She turned as she heard him and paused. 'Mr. Rivington, isn't it?' she asked, and he nodded, looking at her appreciatively. She was dressed in a simple black frock that was anything but new. The short sleeves disclosed the roundness of her arms and the whiteness of her skin, and the sombre hue threw into relief the pale gold of her hair.

'I'm glad you're here, Mr. Rivington,' she whispered. 'My guardian told me that your brother had arranged for you to come down.'

'I hope,' said Bob, 'that my presence won't be necessary.'

'I hope so, too,' said the woman quickly, and a momentary flash of fear showed in her eyes. 'I'll take you to the dining room.'

She escorted him to a large apartment on the opposite side of the hall to the study. Samuel Coyne, still in his wheelchair, was seated at the head of the table.

'So you've met my ward, Diana,' he said as they came in. 'I hope you found everything upstairs that you required?'

'Yes, thank you,' said Bob politely.

'I'm afraid,' continued Coyne, 'that our habits here are rather spartan, but if there's anything you want please don't hesitate to ask for it. I should like to make your stay as comfortable as possible.'

Bob thought that comfort and The Wilderness were so far removed that the carrying out of this wish would be next to impossible, but he merely thanked his host again and, when Diana had seated herself, took his place at the table.

The meal that followed was one of the worst he had ever eaten. The soup was thin and watery, with lumps of half-congealed fat floating on the surface. The beef, which came after, was undercooked and tough; the vegetables discoloured. A sweet of tinned fruit and cream was the best part of the dinner, and Bob was heartily glad when the coffee stage was reached.

Throughout the meal, conversation had flagged. The host was gloomy and absent-minded, and although Bob tried to enter into a discussion with Diana, she answered only in monosyllables, and he eventually gave up the attempt. There was a difference in her attitude from that when he had met her in the hall. The presence of her guardian seemed to act like a blanket. He saw her every now and again, when she made one of her few remarks, shoot a little furtive glance in his direction as though expecting his disapproval. Altogether a queer establishment, he thought.

'You'll excuse me,' said Coyne, when he had gulped down his coffee quickly, 'if I leave you, but I have some work to do.'

'Don't worry about me, Mr. Coyne,' said Bob readily, rather glad than otherwise that the man was going.

'Diana will look after you,' said Coyne, wheeling his chair skilfully and rapidly to the door. 'If I don't see you again, I wish you good night.' Bob got up to open the door for him, and he propelled himself out.

'How long do these fits of rheumatism last?' he asked as he closed the door and resumed his seat at the table.

Diana blew out the match with which she had just lighted a cigarette and dropped it onto her plate. 'They vary,' she answered. 'Sometimes a week, sometimes longer.'

'And during the attacks, is he quite unable to move?' he enquired.

'Quite,' she replied. 'Gunter has to carry him up to bed and down in the morning.'

'It must be very unpleasant,' said Bob. 'Particularly as I understand that when he's free from these attacks, he's more or less an active man.'

'Yes. I think it may have a great deal to do with his irritability,' she replied. 'Tell me, how long are you going to stay?'

'I don't know. Until my brother recalls me, I suppose.'

'It's nice to have someone in the house. You don't know how — how scared I've been during the last few weeks.'

He seized the opportunity that the opening offered. 'Do you know anything about these attacks on your guardian?'

'What do you mean?' she said sharply.

'I mean, have you any idea what's behind them?'

'Oh, I see. No, I know nothing,' she declared.

'You can think of no reason for someone wishing to injure Mr. Coyne?' he persisted.

'No reason at all.'

'It seems very peculiar,' he continued. 'Mr. Coyne can apparently suggest no motive for these attempts on his life, and yet there must be one. People don't go about trying to kill other people without a reason.'

She was uneasy; he saw that in the way she avoided his eyes. 'No, I suppose not,' she agreed. 'But I assure you, Mr. Rivington, that I have no idea why anyone should wish to harm my guardian.'

He remembered the discovery Paul had made concerning the sender of the telegram, and wondered. Did Diana know something that she was keeping back? His brother had been explicit in his instructions that Bob was not to let her know that the origin of the telegram had been discovered, and therefore he thought it best not to refer to it.

'The last attempt was made, I understand,' he said, 'two nights ago when someone shot at Mr. Coyne in the garden. Did you hear anything of that?'

'No, I was out,' she answered.

'And the servants?' he continued. 'They must have heard the shot?'

'They were out, too.'

'You'll forgive me questioning you, Miss Fielding,' he continued after a pause, 'but I want to get as much information about this business as possible. The more I know about it, the easier it'll be for me to carry out my job.'

'I'm sorry, but I can't think of anything else to tell you.'

'This servant of yours, Gunter — is he to be entirely trusted?'

She looked at him for the first time during their brief conversation. 'Why do you ask that?' she enquired.

'Because personally I've taken rather a dislike to him.'

'I don't know anything about him,' she replied, frowning. 'He's not a good servant, he's abrupt, and sometimes rather rude, but he's strong, and I think that's the reason my guardian engaged him. He's useful when these attacks come on and Mr. Coyne can't move.'

'Has he been with you long?' asked Bob.

She thought for a moment before replying. 'Nearly — six months,' she said at length. 'Perhaps — ' She rose abruptly to her feet. ' — you'd like to see the system of alarms my guardian's installed. He asked me to show them to you.'

He realised that she was making an effort to change the conversation, and since its continuance seemed unlikely to yield anything useful, he fell in with her wishes. 'Yes, I should,' he said simply.

She took him round the house, showing him the various alarms that had been fixed in the different rooms. 'They work from wires,' she explained, 'which Gunter sets last thing before going to bed.'

He listened in silence. These elaborate precautions, would they have been taken to keep out an *unknown* enemy? Personally he thought it very unlikely. The danger of which Samuel Coyne was afraid was not the danger of the unknown, but the *known*. The fear in the man's eyes, the locked gates, the alarms and trip-wires — everything tended to confirm this. He knew very well who it was who sought his life and why, and the knowledge instilled in him the terror which Bob had more than once surprised in his face. But if he knew, if he was aware of the true meaning of this menace, why didn't he say so? Why did he steadfastly assert that he had no knowledge of the person responsible for the three attempts to kill him?

There was only one logical explanation for this — because he dared not. Because by doing so, he would bring upon himself a greater danger than the one he feared. Bob was becoming interested. The situation appealed to his imagination, and counteracted to a large extent the unpleasant discomfort of the house.

He saw no more of Samuel Coyne that night. The rest of the evening he spent talking to Diana in the shabby drawing-room, and once off the subject of Samuel Coyne and his fears, she became less reticent. The restraint she had put upon herself wore off, and by the time the evening came to a close, she was almost cheerful.

Bob had brought a book with him, and for some time before going bed he sat reading, but his mind was not entirely concentrated on the story. He heard Coyne being carried up to bed, and later Gunter making a round of the house and locking up, and then gradually silence descended upon the place; a silence that was broken only by the sighing of the rising wind and the gentle patter of the rain.

It was midnight when he laid aside his book and, undressing, got into bed. For some time he lay awake staring into the darkness, wondering what solution lay behind this curious affair in which he had become involved.

Sleep came to him suddenly. One moment he was pondering over the fear of Samuel Coyne, and the next he had slid imperceptibly into unconsciousness. And then without warning he was wide awake and sitting up in bed, his ears filled with a loud buzzing. The alarm above his head was ringing violently.

6

The Man in the Garden

He slipped quickly out of bed and shuffled over to the window. Pulling aside the curtains, he peered out. The darkness was intense and he could see nothing. The buzzer above his bed, however, continued to vibrate angrily. Someone had gained admission to the grounds, accidentally come into contact with one of the wires, and set off the alarm.

Hastily he pulled on a pair of trousers, thrust his feet into his slippers, and grabbed the pistol he had laid in readiness on the table by his bedside. Opening the door, he stepped out into the dark passage and listened. There was no sound. The rest of the household had apparently not been disturbed. He thought this was peculiar, since from what he had seen of the system, the alarms rang in every room simultaneously.

He made his way swiftly to the landing and began to descend the stairs. As he reached the bottom, his hand touched something soft and warm, and his heart bounded into his mouth. He heard a stifled exclamation, and the hand he had touched gripped his wrist.

'Who's that?' growled a husky whisper, and it was with relief that he recognised the voice of Gunter.

'It's all right — it's me, Mr. Rivington,' said Bob. 'I heard the alarm, and — '

'I heard it, too,' growled the servant. 'There's somebody outside in the garden. I was going to see who, but as you're here, you can do that. I'll go up and look after the guv'nor. There's a buzzer in his room and it must have wakened him. I expect he's half dead with fright.' He added the last contemptuously, and Bob heard the stairs creak as he left him and began to make his way to the floor above. He crossed the hall, fumbled for the bolts that fastened the front door, and pulled them back as noiselessly as he could. Opening it softly, he stepped out into the darkness.

The night was chill and it was raining. Descending the shallow flight of steps, he stood on the gravel of the path and listened. No sound came to him from the back of the house, and stealthily he made his way round the angle of the wall.

The desolate garden, shrouded in darkness, lay before him, but there was no sight or sound of movement. He paused irresolutely. It was useless giving evidence of his presence until he knew something of the direction in which he was likely to find the lurking intruder. And then sounds came to him: the rustle of bushes and the snapping of a twig. Straining his eyes to pierce the darkness, he caught a glimpse of a blot of shadow moving among the other shadows of the garden. Cautiously, he began to creep towards it. His foot came down on a dead branch and it snapped with a loud crack that was magnified by the surrounding stillness.

The shadow in front stopped, and he heard a muffled oath. Realising that it was useless trying to conceal his presence any longer, he sprang forward.

The unknown marauder took to his

heels, and Bob went after him. His eyes had got accustomed to the darkness now, and he could see the flying figure of his quarry speeding across the rank lawn. It was doubtful, with the start the other had, if Bob could have caught up with him but for a lucky chance. The running man's flying feet caught in one of the trip-wires and he fell sprawling. Before he could scramble to his feet, Bob had reached him and ground the muzzle of his pistol into his neck.

'Now then,' he panted, 'you try any tricks and I'll blow your head to pieces!' He had no intention of carrying out his horrifying threat, but it had the desired effect. His prisoner gave a gasp of alarm.

''Ere, you be careful with that thing!' he whined. 'I ain't goin' to make no trouble. It's a fair cop.' Bob hauled him to his feet. He was a small undersized man, and made no effort to put up a fight.

'What are you doing on these premises?' demanded Bob sternly.

'I ain't doin' no 'arm,' whined his prisoner. 'Just lookin' fer somewhere to doss. You don't want to be too 'ad,

73

guv'nor. I ain't 'ad a square meal fer three days, and I thought p'raps I could find a bed or somethin' where I could lie down out of the wet and get some sleep.'

'You'll find the cells at the police station nice and dry,' snapped Bob. 'Come on back to the house. I want to have a look at you.'

His captive offered no resistance. He appeared to have accepted the position philosophically, due most probably to his evident fear of the automatic in Bob's hand. He took him back to the front entrance and thrust him into the darkened hall. Following, he felt for the switch and pressed it down. As the hall became flooded with light, he took a look at the other's ferret-like face, and his lips pursed themselves into a whistle.

'So it's you,' he said. 'I thought you were still in prison, Weepers.'

'Blimey, fancy runnin' into you 'ere,' said the little man disconsolately. 'What a bit o' bad luck!'

Bob smiled. Alf Weepers was the last person he had expected to see. He was a burglar, and not a very clever one, as the string of convictions attached to his name in the record office at Scotland Yard testified.

'What are you goin' to do?' said Mr. Weepers anxiously. 'There ain't no call to bother the perlice, is there? I ain't done no 'arm.'

'Trespassing on enclosed premises with criminal intent,' said Bob curtly. 'You'll get another nine months for this, Weepers, if the magistrate's in a good temper.'

'I've never met a beak in a good temper yet,' said Mr. Weepers scornfully, and at that moment Gunter appeared at the head of the stairs.

'Did you catch him?' he called.

'Yes,' said Bob. 'I've got him here. He's not very alarming, just an ordinary burglar and about as dangerous as a tame cat. Is Mr. Coyne awake?'

'Yes,' said the servant. 'I'll fetch him down.'

He disappeared, and Weepers turned to Bob. 'Who's Coyne?' he asked. 'Is he the boss of this place?'

Bob nodded.

'I always was unlucky,' grumbled the burglar self-pityingly. I've 'ad me eye on this place for a couple o' nights. Thought it was cinch, and now look at me.'

Bob's mouth twitched. Mr. Weepers' appearance was so forlorn, his expression so dejected, that it was almost ludicrous. He had expected to find a desperate man lurking in the shadows of the garden, and the reality was so contrary to his expectation that the situation was humorous.

'Who is it? Who set off the alarm?' The quavering, frightened voice of Samuel Coyne came to Bob's ears, and looking round he saw the master of the house being carried down the stairs by Gunter.

'It's all right, Mr. Coyne,' said Bob reassuringly. 'It's nothing to be alarmed about. It was just an ordinary attempt at burglary, nothing more serious. I've got the fellow here; he's well known to the police. If you ring up the station, they'll send a man round and collect him.'

The wheelchair was standing near the

foot of the staircase, and Gunter deposited his employer in it. 'Who is he? What's his name?' demanded Mr. Coyne, wheeling himself rapidly forward.

Before Bob could answer, Mr. Weepers uttered an exclamation. 'Blimey!' he breathed in astonishment. 'Kilroe!'

The effect of his words on Coyne was remarkable. The man's face went a dirty grey, and he stared with bulging eyes at the figure of the crook. For a moment his lips moved soundlessly, and then he found his voice. 'I'll deal with this man,' he said huskily, speaking with difficulty. 'There's no need to drag the police into this matter.'

Bob saw a smile curve the lips of Mr. Weepers. 'But — ' he began.

'I'll deal with him, I tell you!' repeated Coyne impatiently. 'Obviously he's got nothing to do with the other matter, and we don't want to make trouble. Come into my study.' He addressed the last part of his remark to Mr. Weepers, and the man strutted after him as he wheeled himself rapidly across the hall. Bob watched, full of amazement, as he disappeared within the room followed by the burglar, and the door shut behind them.

The episode of the night had taken on a queer aspect. Bob bit his lip irritably. He was annoyed at this high-handed action on the part of his host. The watchful Gunter saw his annoyance and smiled sourly.

'Full of courage now, ain't you?' he said with a sneer, jerking his thumb in the direction of the closed door of the study. 'You should 'ave seen 'im a little while ago. When I went in to him, he was so frightened he was like a jellyfish.'

Bob had no wish to discuss Coyne with the servant, and changed the subject. 'We seem to have had our alarm for nothing,' he said. 'How's Miss Fielding?'

'I ain't seen nothing of her,' Gunter replied. 'There ain't an alarm in her room, so it's more than likely she's still sleeping.'

Bob thought this was distinctly unlikely. The capture of Mr. Weepers had resulted in a considerable noise. Surely Diana had heard something, though perhaps she preferred to keep to her room. What had the burglar meant by addressing Coyne as Kilroe? That was the queerest part of the night's performance. Had he made a mistake, or had he really recognised Coyne? Bob was inclined to believe the latter, for he remembered the extraordinary change in the man's expression when the name had left the thief's lips. In which case, Kilroe was his real name and Coyne was an alias. The more he saw of this strange business, the fishier it became.

There was a faint murmur of voices from behind the study door, but he could hear nothing of what was being said. He lingered, however, determined to see the events of that night to their finish; and he hadn't long to wait. A few more minutes passed and then the door of the study opened. Mr. Weepers came out, followed by Coyne in his wheelchair. The thief's thin weasel-like face was radiant.

'I don't think we need go to any more trouble over this man,' said Coyne. 'He admits that he came here with intent to steal, but I've listened to his story and it seems he's had a pretty bad time lately. I don't want to make it worse for him. I think the best thing we can do is to let him go.'

'That's entirely up to you,' Bob said with a shrug. 'Though personally, I should send for the police and have him locked up. He's a dangerous character, and if he's left to go free it means that someone else will shortly become parted from their property.'

'You ain't got no call to go puttin' your oar in!' said Mr. Weepers, scowling at him. 'If the — guv'nor 'ere says I can go, it means there ain't no charge, see!'

'Perhaps I'm being a little stupid,' apologised Coyne. 'But the fact of the matter is, I hate sending a fellow creature to prison.'

'Very kind of yer,' whined Mr. Weepers, 'and I appreciates it.'

The look on Coyne's face was hardly consistent with the magnanimous attitude he had adopted, for he shot a glance at the burglar that was murderous.

'I won't keep you up,' said Mr. Weepers generously, moving towards the door. 'I'll just thank you kindly again, sir, and make myself scarce.'

Coyne watched him until he had disappeared into the darkness of the night, then he looked at Bob. 'I've no doubt you think I've behaved foolishly,' he said. 'But he told me a very pathetic story, and — '

'It's part of his stock-in-trade,' said Bob curtly. 'It's nothing to do with me, Mr. Coyne. If you like to let him go, that's your business.'

'It would have meant a lot of trouble and unpleasantness to charge him,' explained Mr. Coyne. 'I should have had to appear and — well, I'd rather let the matter drop. He hasn't done any harm.'

'He didn't get much chance!' retorted Bob. 'I think I'll go back to bed, if you don't mind. There doesn't seem to be any reason for remaining up.'

'Please don't think I'm ungrateful,' said Coyne anxiously. 'I must thank you for the promptness with which you acted. Has anyone seen my ward?' He looked from Bob to Gunter, and it was the servant who answered.

'Ain't seen nothing of her,' he grunted.

Coyne frowned. 'Go and see what's happened to her,' he said sharply. 'She's sure to be awake; she couldn't have slept through all this noise.'

The servant shrugged his shoulders, and for a moment Bob thought he was going to refuse. Then, muttering something below his breath, he turned towards the staircase and began to mount it slowly.

Coyne, the frown still on his face, looked across at the open front door and shivered. 'D'you mind shutting it?' he asked. 'I'm sorry to trouble you, but in my present state I can't do it myself.'

Bob complied with the request in silence. He was still annoyed, and his annoyance must have shown in his face, for Coyne reopened the subject of Mr. Weepers in a conciliatory voice.

'I feel,' he said, 'that you rather resent my action in letting that fellow go?'

'I think you acted unwisely,' said Bob curtly. 'But as I said before, it's your business. You arranged for me to come down and protect you from an unknown menace, and when I find a man prowling about on the grounds, you let him go.'

'He can't have had anything to do with the other matter.'

'How do you know that?' broke in Bob. 'You yourself affirm that you have no knowledge of who's at the bottom of these attempts on your life. How do you know Weepers isn't an emissary of the unknown person who's tried to kill you three times?'

For a moment the other looked nonplussed and a little uneasy. 'You don't — you don't think he could be?' he muttered.

'Why not? He's a crook with a string of convictions to his name. He's not a killer, but he's capable of anything short of murder. Why shouldn't he be in the employ of this person you're afraid of?'

'There's something in what you say.' Coyne's face was troubled. 'Perhaps it was silly of me to let him go after all.'

'That's a mistake that can easily be rectified,' said Bob. 'Let me get on to the local police now and tell them he's in the neighbourhood. They'll soon pull him in and — '

'No, no!' Coyne held up his hand. 'I won't go back on my word. I told him I'd let him go, and I'll stick to it.'

Bob was satisfied. He had learned just what he had wanted to know. As frightened as Samuel Coyne was of the unknown, his fear was not great enough to overcome an equal fear of what Mr. Weepers might say. The burglar knew something about this man who sat huddled up in the invalid chair; knew something that Coyne dreaded he might divulge, and it was for this reason he had let him go.

Gunter came down the stairs quickly at that moment. 'Miss Fielding's not in her room,' he announced.

Coyne sat up with a jerk. 'Not in her room? What d'you mean? Where is she?'

'How do I know where she is? All I can tell you is that she ain't in her room.'

'She must be!' snapped Coyne angrily. 'Unless she's somewhere else in the house.'

'Well, go and look for her yourself!' said Gunter rudely.

'You go, will you?' asked Coyne, looking at Bob; and with a nod he hurried up the stairs.

'Which is Miss Fielding's room?' he called from the landing.

'Second door down the left-hand passage,' replied Coyne, and Bob turned in this direction.

He had no difficulty in finding the room, for the door was open and the light was on. One glance showed him that the room was empty and also that the bed was smooth and undisturbed. It had never been slept in.

He came back to the hall and reported his discovery. Coyne's face flushed with anger. 'Where the devil can she be?' he exclaimed, and raising his voice called: 'Diana! Diana!' But there was no reply. 'Search the house!' he ordered querulously. 'She must be here somewhere.'

But although Bob and Gunter went through the place from roof to cellar, there was no sign of Diana Fielding. She had disappeared.

7

A Paragraph in a Paper

The discovery that Diana was no longer in the house acted on Coyne like the proverbial red rag to the popular bull. His swarthy face flushed and the veins in his temples stood out with the rage which he strove ineffectually to conceal. Bob got a glimpse in that moment of what the man was really like, and the revelation was not pleasant.

'Where can she have gone?' he stormed, thumping his clenched fist on the arm of his wheelchair. 'Where can she have gone? She had no right to go out! She had no right to leave the house without my permission.'

'What's the good of getting in a temper?' growled Gunter. 'That won't do no good. She's gone, and all the raving in the world won't bring her back.'

'She must be found!' snarled Coyne.

'In my state of health, I can't get on without her.'

'Does she have any friends she may have gone to?' asked Bob.

Coyne shook his head. 'No. Besides, would she choose the middle of the night to visit them? See if she's taken anything with her.'

Bob might have resented his tone if he hadn't been so intensely interested and puzzled about this disappearance. Where *had* she gone? He went upstairs, accompanied by the surly-faced servant, and made a closer examination of her room. An inspection of the wardrobe revealed that it was empty, as were the drawers of the dressing chest. It was Gunter who pointed out that the suitcase which usually occupied a position at the foot of the bed was missing. 'She's scooted,' he said with conviction. 'And I don't blame her. He was always on at her about one thing or another, and I suppose she got fed up and cleared out.'

'Rather a peculiar time to choose, don't you think?' suggested Bob, frowning. 'She must have waited until everyone was in bed and asleep.'

'I suppose she thought he'd stop her if he knew she was going. And he would, too! Wonder if she's taken the car?'

He went downstairs, followed by Bob, and opened the back door. The garage was built onto the side of the house, and making their way round to it, Gunter took a key from his pocket and unlocked the heavy door.

'The car's still here,' he muttered, pointing to the ancient machine. 'She must have gone on foot.'

'How big was the suitcase?' asked Bob.

'Fair size. Why?'

'I was thinking that it must have been pretty heavy for her to manage.'

Gunter shrugged. 'She didn't have many things. Coyne saw to that.'

'She must have gone after you'd locked up,' continued Bob. 'How did she get out? Did you find anything open?'

'I ain't looked,' was the reply. 'P'raps we'd better see.' They made a round of the house. A small window in the scullery was unlatched, and beneath it were the prints of high-heeled shoes.

'That's the way she got out,' said Bob, pointing. 'Let's see if we can find which way she went.'

The gravel was soft with the rain, and the heel marks were distinctly visible. They followed them round to the front of the house and down the drive. At the closed gates, they branched off through a patch of shrubbery to the foot of the high wall. Bob frowned. It was fairly evident that Diana had climbed the wall at this point, but how had she managed to do so without assistance?

'Have you got the key of the gate?' he asked.

Gunter nodded.

'I'd like to have a look round outside.'

Grumbling, the servant unlocked the heavy gate; and passing through, Bob made his way round to the other side of the wall where the footprints had ended. By the light of his torch, he found further traces easily, and with them the mark of another foot — the larger footprint of a man. He also found something else.

A yard or two away from the place was

a patch of black that gleamed darkly on the wet surface of the road — oil! That, and the marks of tyres which were clearly visible, told him that a car had waited there. Evidently Diana Fielding hadn't gone alone. Somebody with a car had been waiting for her — had in all probability assisted her over the high wall, which, encumbered by her suitcase, it would have been next to impossible for her to have climbed alone.

He mentioned these discoveries to the beetle-browed Gunter, who whistled. 'Went off with someone, did she? You wait till he hears that. That'll please him, I don't think! I wonder who it could have been?'

Bob was not in a position to offer any suggestion, and they went back to the house. Samuel Coyne had wheeled himself into his little study and was sitting staring gloomily at the dead embers in the grate. As Gunter had prophesied, his reception of Bob's discoveries was another burst of fury.

'Had a man with her, did she?' he shouted. 'So that's what she's been doing, has she? Meeting some fellow on the sly and pitching tales about the hard way she was treated. I'll have something to say when she comes back! I'll punish her for this. I'm her legal guardian, and she's no right to go without my permission!'

'What do you intend to do about it?' asked Bob coldly. His sympathies at that moment were entirely with the missing woman. If she had to put up with much of this sort of thing, he was not surprised she had gone.

'What can I do about it?' snarled Coyne. 'I can't move, I'm helpless.'

'You could notify the police,' suggested Bob, but the other waved away the suggestion impatiently.

'I don't want to drag the police into my private affairs,' he said, swallowing his anger with an effort. 'If that's all the gratitude she feels for everything I've done for her, let her go!'

Bob was undeceived by this sudden change of front. Coyne was still as incensed as ever at Diane's action. Beneath his forced calm, there were still traces to be seen of the rage that seethed within him, though the mention of the police had reduced his hectoring tone to a mildness that was as spurious as it was sudden. A thought struck Bob, and he turned to Gunter.

'What about the maid?' he said. 'It's curious she should have slept through all this.'

'She don't sleep here,' was the surly answer. 'She comes in the morning, and she leaves again at night.'

'She lives in the village,' augmented Samuel Coyne. 'Make some coffee will you, Gunter?'

Once again, Bob thought the man was going to refuse; and then, muttering something beneath his breath, he slouched away. There was a silence after he had gone, broken at last by Coyne.

'This is all very unpleasant,' he said deprecatingly. 'I really must apologise for this unexpected disturbance on your first night here.'

He was evidently trying to counteract any unfavourable impression he may have created by his previous outburst. 'There's no need to apologise, Mr. Coyne,' said

Bob a little formally. 'This disturbance wasn't under your control and you couldn't help it. Anyway, I came down in the expectation of something of the sort.'

'Yes, yes, of course. I'm extremely glad to have you here. Moreso than ever now that my ward has deserted me. Gunter's all very well, but he's an uncouth brute, and by no stretch of the imagination could he be called a congenial companion.'

Bob wondered who *could* be a congenial companion to Mr. Samuel Coyne, and decided that it was a question that required a great deal of consideration. The dislike he had experienced on first meeting this man was growing stronger with every moment spent in his company. When he wasn't raging he was whining, and the combination was not edifying.

Gunter came back with a tray of coffee and set it down with a clatter on the corner of the desk. 'There y'are,' he muttered. 'And if there's nothing else you want, I'd like to get a bit more sleep.' He didn't wait for Coyne's reply, but shuffled over to the door and went out without another word. They heard his heavy footsteps ascending the stairs, followed soon after by the slam of a door.

'I suppose we may as well follow his example when we've had this,' said Coyne, twisting his chair round towards the desk and pouring out the coffee, 'though it won't be long before morning.'

The sky outside was already lightening. It was a cold grey light against which the gaunt branches of the trees showed up blackly. Bob, who was cold and tired, gulped the scalding liquid the servant had hastily prepared. 'Can I help you?' he asked, realising that his host was power-less to climb the stairs by himself; but Coyne shook his head.

'No, I shan't bother to go back to bed,' he said. 'I'll doze here. If you'll give me that rug — ' He nodded to a thick travelling rug that hung over the back of a chair. ' — I shall be all right.'

'You're sure?' persisted Bob. 'I can easily — '

'No, no, I shall be all right, I tell you,' broke in Coyne impatiently with a momentary return of ill humour. 'Give me the rug and clear off to bed.'

Bob gave it to him and watched him while he tucked it round his legs, and then made his way up to his room and his disturbed rest. He made no effort to remove the clothing he had hastily assumed at the first sound of the alarm, but lying down on the bed, pulled the coverlet over him and stared into the semidarkness.

Although he was tired, he found it difficult to sleep. The events of the night came crowding back to his brain, keeping him wakeful. It was a queer business, he thought — queer but interesting. Why was Coyne passing under a name that was not his own? Because he was afraid of someone, or because he was afraid of the law? He found it difficult to make up his mind which of these was the true explanation. There was no doubt that Samuel Coyne was terrified, and his terror was the terror of death. Bob had seen that fear of fears in too many men's eyes not to recognise it. But he was also afraid of something else. From his very definite reluctance to come in contact with the police, Bob concluded that this secondary fear was concerned with something he had done that would put him within reach of the law. The burglar, Alf Weepers, had addressed him as Kilroe, and he tried to recollect if he had ever heard the name before, but he couldn't remember having done so. The effect of it on Coyne, however, had been remarkable. Never before had Bob seen such an abject expression of terror come into any man's face as when the burglar had uttered his exclamation of recognition. He made a mental note to report that episode to his brother and see whether the name Kilroe conveyed anything to Paul.

His thoughts switched to Diana Fielding. During his conversation with her, he hadn't noticed anything that suggested she was on the point running away. Either she had made up her mind very suddenly, which seemed absurd in view of the car and the man who had helped her to scale that wall, or she was an expert at concealing her emotions. There would have been no opportunity for her to communicate with anyone during the evening, for the telephone was in Coyne's study, so any arrangement she had made for leaving must have been carried out early in the day. Unless — a thought struck him — unless the maid had been the messenger.

It would have been quite possible for her to have delivered a note on her way home. He wondered whether this was what had actually happened, but he couldn't bring himself to believe that Diana had had any idea of leaving the house when they had sat talking in the dining-room. The decision had been sudden and abrupt. Whatever had promoted it had happened after she had left him and gone up to her room. In which case, it could not have been the maid who had taken the message to the unknown man who had helped her. And why had she gone at all? Was it because she was unhappy with Samuel Coyne? That was quite believable; but still, there was nothing to show that his habits had altered so much recently as to offer an explanation for her sudden departure. If there was another reason, what was it? What had happened to send her suddenly fleeing from the house in the middle of a cold and rainy night?

He fell asleep while he was still conjecturing about the motive for her extraordinary action, and when he awoke again it was to find the daylight streaming through the window and the maid at his bedside with a cup of tea. He swallowed it, his eyes still heavy with sleep, and getting out of bed pulled on his dressing gown and went over to the window.

It was still raining — a drab, cheerless-looking morning — and with a shiver he picked up a towel preparatory to making his way to the bathroom. His eyes were hot, and he was still weary from his disturbed night, and the prospects of spending a day in this gloomy house did nothing to raise his spirits.

He had opened the door and stepped out into the passage when a hoarse inarticulate cry reached his ears from somewhere below. It was a cry of such stark terror that his blood froze, and turning, he flew to the head of the staircase.

'What is it? What's the matter?' he called sharply.

'It's Mr. Coyne! He's had a fit or something!' answered the surly tones of Gunter; and running down the stairs, Bob saw the frightened maid standing at the open door of the study.

Going over quickly, he looked in. Gunter was bending over the wheelchair in which Coyne sprawled limply, his face livid, his head sunk on his chest. In his clenched hand was a crumpled newspaper he had evidently been reading at the time of his seizure.

'Open the window, and get some brandy!' ordered Bob, loosening the unconscious man's collar. 'And you'd better telephone for a doctor. Is he subject to these attacks?'

The servant shook his head. He ain't never had one so long as I've been here,' he growled, and proceeded to carry out Bob's instructions.

He opened the window letting in a flood of cold air, and going away, presently returned with a half-full bottle of brandy and a glass. Bob splashed some of the spirit into the tumbler and forced a few drops between Coyne's lips. As he was putting the glass on the table, he happened to catch sight of a paragraph in the newspaper. It was headed:

MYSTERIOUS CRIME AT HAMPSTEAD

'UNKNOWN MAN WITH SHAVEN HEAD FOUND MURDERED ON SPANIARDS ROAD.'

He frowned. Was that what Coyne had been reading when the fit had taken him? And if so, was it the reason for that strange and sudden attack?

8

Rivington is Puzzled

It was late when Paul reached home after the discovery of the shaven man on the side of Spaniards Road, and later still before he finally went to bed. The crime on which he had accidentally stumbled interested him, and he sat up for a long time thinking it over.

The queer feature of the shaven head fascinated him. Why had the man's head been shaved? What possible reason could there be behind such a grotesque action on the part of the murderer? Had it been done with some vague idea of preventing identification? That had been the first thought that had occurred to him, but such a solution appeared, for several reasons, unsatisfactory. There were other ways of achieving the same result more certainly. The removal of the hair would not alter the features, and although to a

101

great extent it would change his appearance, it would not do so sufficiently to prevent recognition by anyone who knew him.

That, of course, was the first step towards clearing up the mystery. Until the man had been identified, he had no beginning, no life into which enquiries could be made with the object of discovering a possible motive for his death.

Paul was convinced from his inspection of the dead man's hands that he was not a tramp, as his appearance seemed to suggest. The softness of the skin in no way tallied with the grimy clothing. It was not unreasonable, therefore, to conclude that he was disguised, which only added a deeper mystery to the affair.

It was a fascinating problem; fascinating because of its strangeness. Here was a man, obviously murdered, left at the side of a lonely road, with his head shaved of every particle of hair and not the remotest clue to his identity. The ashtray by Paul's side was filled with cigarette stubs before he rose with a yawn and went to bed, having come to the conclusion that until more details concerning the dead man came to light, it was useless trying to conjecture the motive for his death.

He was up early on the following morning. Only one newspaper carried an account of the discovery, and this was very brief. Paul guessed — and was right, as it happened — that a reporter must have been at the police station when the news came through, otherwise the information would never have reached *The Megaphone* in time for the morning edition.

He had finished his breakfast and was dealing with his mail when his servant announced the arrival of Inspector Robin. The beady-eyed, round-faced little man came quickly into the room, peeling off his dripping mackintosh and depositing it with his hat on a chair.

'You're an early bird, Robin,' remarked Paul, smiling. 'What worm are you after?'

Round Robin warmed his chubby hands at the fire. 'I've been put in charge of this Hampstead murder, Mr. Rivington,' he said in his piping voice, 'and I've come round to have a chat with you about it. You were present when the discovery was made, weren't you?'

Paul got up from his desk, went over to the mantelpiece, and helped himself to a cigarette. 'I was,' he said. 'An extraordinary affair. What do you make of it?'

'I don't make anything of it,' Mr. Robin said with a shrug. 'I came round to see if you had any suggestions to offer me.'

Paul lit his cigarette carefully and flicked the match into the grate. 'I'm afraid I haven't at the moment. Have you succeeded in identifying the dead man?'

'No,' the inspector answered gloomily. 'That's the trouble. Until we can do that, we've got nowhere to start.'

'And I've an idea,' murmured Paul, blowing out a cloud of smoke, 'that you're not going to find it too easily. Either the dead man himself, or his murderer, went to the greatest possible trouble to remove anything by which his identity could be traced.'

'Even to shaving his head,' murmured Mr. Robin.

'Maybe you're right, but I'm not at all sure about that.'

The inspector shot him a quick glance. 'You've got some other idea to account for it?'

'No,' said Paul, 'but I'm under the impression that it wasn't done to make identification difficult.'

'Then why *was* it done? What other reason could the murderer have had for shaving off all his victim's hair?'

'I don't know.' Paul's expression was thoughtful. 'I think if we knew that, we should be a long way towards knowing why he was killed.'

'You mean it might have something to do with the motive for the crime?' said Round Robin, rubbing his smooth chin. 'I don't see how.'

'I don't, either. But it seems to me a more probable suggestion than that it was done to conceal his identity. There are so many things that would have been more effectual. The murderer could have damaged the features in such a way as to make them unrecognisable.'

'Hm, yes!' The inspector's tone was

doubtful. 'Still, I don't see what motive can include the shaving of a man's head, unless the killer was a lunatic.'

'That's not impossible.'

'You think he was a homicidal maniac, eh?' asked Mr. Robin quickly. 'Well, you may be right.'

'I didn't say I thought anything of the sort! I merely said it wasn't impossible. It might be the crime of a religious fanatic, someone who belongs to a sect in which the shaven head is part of a ritual. Such things have been known. There are any number of suggestions to account for it. But it won't do any good wasting time on pure speculation. The first thing to do is to discover who the dead man was; then we've got something to work on.'

'Well, we've been through all the lists of missing people, and none of them remotely resemble this fellow.'

'It's probable he hasn't been missing long enough to be included in your list. I suppose you're adopting the usual procedure?'

Round Robin nodded. 'A post-mortem photograph of the man has been taken, and that and his description will be circulated throughout the country. The negative was retouched by our expert to make him look as much as possible as he would have done before his hair was removed.'

'It's quite possible you may get results,' said Paul, but his tone was not very optimistic. 'Somebody must know the man, and probably they'll come forward. If you do hear anything, I wish you'd let me know.'

'You bet your life I will!' promised Mr. Robin.

He took his departure shortly after, more than a little disappointed at the result of his visit. At the back of his mind had been a lurking hope that his friend would have proved more helpful.

Paul returned to his interrupted mail, and he had just finished scribbling notes for his reply to the last letter when Bob came in. 'Hello!' said his brother, looking up in surprise. 'I didn't expect to see you back so soon. What's happened?'

Bob flung himself wearily into a chair. 'Quite a lot,' he replied.

Paul eyed him critically. He looked tired and worn out. 'You don't look as if you've had much sleep,' he remarked.

Bob made a grimace. 'I've had scarcely any. From my experience, life at Coyne's house is one constant round of excitement.'

'You don't mean,' said Paul quickly, 'that there's been another attempt on the man's life?'

'No. But that's about the only thing that hasn't happened. I'll tell you all about it.'

Briefly, but without omitting any essential details, he gave an account of the night's happenings at The Wilderness, and Paul listened without interruption until he came to the end of his recital, then he pursed his lips and frowned.

'Extraordinary!' he muttered. 'So Coyne's real name is Kilroe, is it?'

'I don't think there's any doubt of it,' said Bob. 'Weepers recognised him instantly. Does the name convey anything to you?'

'Nothing at all, old chap. So far as I can remember, I've never heard it before.'

'I was hoping it might,' said Bob, suppressing a prodigious yawn. 'There's something pretty queer about the whole thing. Coyne is definitely afraid of someone or something, and although he pretends ignorance, it's my belief he knows the reason for these attacks on him.'

'That was my impression, too,' said Paul thoughtfully. 'As you say, it's a queer business. Obviously the reason he was so anxious to let Weepers go was because he was scared of what the man might say. The thing I don't like is this sudden disappearance of his ward. Who was this man who was waiting for her in the car, and why did she choose such an extraordinary time to leave?'

'You've hit on the very thing that puzzles me,' said Bob. 'I'm pretty certain she had no intention of going when I left her in the drawing-room and went to bed.'

'And yet,' mused Paul, 'from what you tell me, nobody could have communicated with her after that.'

'It would have been quite impossible,'

declared his brother. 'Anybody attempting to pass through the grounds would have set off one of the alarms.'

'So something must have occurred,' murmured Paul, 'after you'd all gone to bed, to bring about this sudden decision on her part to leave house.'

'It seems like it.'

'But before we can accept that, we've got to explain the man and the car. His presence looks like a definite arrangement. He couldn't possibly have been there waiting on the off-chance that she'd decide to pack up and leave.'

'No,' Bob said with a shrug. 'But perhaps I'm wrong. Perhaps she decided she was going earlier in the day and made all arrangements. After all, I'm only going on her general behaviour during the evening, and it didn't suggest to me that she was contemplating running away.'

'Well, you're in a better position to judge about that than I am,' said Paul. 'But I don't like it all the same. How was Coyne when you left?'

'He'd recovered from his fit, or whatever it was, and definitely refused to see the doctor I insisted should be sent for. Personally, I don't think this attack was anything serious; merely a rather prolonged fainting fit brought on by shock, I think.'

'But what induced the shock?'

Bob's eyes narrowed. 'Well, I'm not sure. But I believe it was caused by something he'd read in the morning newspaper.'

'In the paper, eh?' Paul looked interested.

'Yes, it was in his hand when I found him. And on the page he'd been reading was a short account of a murder that happened at Hampstead last night — ' He stopped abruptly as Paul gave vent to a smothered exclamation.

'So you think that was what gave Coyne his shock?' he said. 'That's very interesting. Now, I wonder what Coyne knows about that unknown man who was found dead at the side of Spaniards Road, that the account of his murder should give him such a shock.'

'There was nothing to prove it was that,' said Bob quickly. 'I'm only guessing.'

'And I think you're guessing right,' replied Paul. He had risen to his feet and was pacing restlessly up and down the room.

'Do you know anything about this murder then?' asked Bob, eyeing him curiously.

'All there is to know, which isn't much. I was there when the body was discovered.' He told his brother how he had come to be mixed up in the affair, and Bob listened interestedly.

'I believe Coyne knows something about it,' he commented when Paul had finished. 'Though what, I haven't any idea. There was nothing else in the paper I could see that was likely to send him into a faint.'

'And there was no mention of the man's name,' said Paul, 'and only a very brief description. Nothing, in fact, to suggest to Coyne who he was or anything about him, except the fact that his head had been shaved.' He stopped and looked at Bob steadily. 'Yes, that was it. If that paragraph was the cause of his attack, it was *not* because he read that an unknown man had been found murdered, but because he he'd been found murdered *with his head shaved.'*

'Why should it scare him into a fit?'

'Because,' said Paul, 'he knows the secret of that shaven head.'

Bob had opened his lips to reply when there came a tap on the door, and in answer to Paul's 'Come in', the maid entered.

'There's a lady to see you, sir,' she announced.

'A lady — what's her name?' asked Paul irritably, a little annoyed at this sudden interruption.

'Mrs. Kilroe, sir,' answered the servant; and Paul Rivington was so astonished that it was some seconds before he could speak.

9

The Man Who Disappeared

'Ask Mrs. Kilroe to come in,' Paul said, and when the maid had departed: 'Peculiar coincidence, eh? If it *is* a coincidence.'

'D'you think this woman can have any connection with Coyne?' Bob enquired.

'I've no idea, but I should think it's quite possible. Kilroe isn't a common name. However, I presume we shall learn who she is and what she wants from her own lips.'

The woman whom the servant presently ushered into the room was stout and impressive. Her face beneath its thick layer of powder was florid and rather masculine. She was dressed in an expensive mink coat that enhanced her bulk, and she stood for a moment in the doorway regarding them through a pair of keen, shrewd eyes.

'Mr. Rivington?' It was a statement rather than a question.

'That's my name,' Paul said, and pushed forward a chair. 'Sit down, Mrs. Kilroe, and tell me how I can assist you.'

She made no immediate effort to comply with the invitation. Her small eyes travelled from Paul to Bob and then back again. 'What I have to say to you, mister,' she said, and her voice was harsh and common, 'is a private matter.'

'Most of the things that are said to me in this room are private matters,' he answered. 'You can speak quite frankly in front of my brother, Mrs. Kilroe; he's entirely in my confidence.'

'That's as may be,' she retorted. 'But I'd rather discuss my business with you alone.'

Bob made a movement to rise, but Paul stopped him with a gesture. 'I'm afraid,' he said a little coldly, 'that whatever you have to say must be said to both of us.'

Her face hardened, and Bob thought for a moment that she was going to walk out, for she made a half-turn towards the door. If this had been her intention, however, she thought better of it.

'Very well,' she said grudgingly. 'If you insist, I suppose it's no good arguing.' She sat down carefully in the chair that Paul had pulled out for her and loosened her coat. 'I want you to clearly understand, though, mister, that what I've come to talk to you about is a private matter. I don't want no publicity or anything like that.'

'Whatever you say to us will go no further, Mrs. Kilroe,' Paul assured her gravely.

'All right, then. As long as that's understood, I'll tell you what I've come about. I want you to find my husband. He's been missing for three days. Went out of the house to post a letter and ain't been back since.'

The idea that had flashed to Paul's mind when she had mentioned the reason for her visit, he instantly discarded. He had imagined for a moment that the missing husband might prove to be the man who called himself Coyne. But the fact that he had only disappeared two nights ago rendered this possibility impracticable. 'Perhaps you could give me some further particulars?' he suggested.

'I doubt there's much I can tell you except that he's disappeared,' she answered. 'Just walked out of the house and vanished into thin air, as you might say. I've been so worried I haven't known what to do or which way to turn.'

'You've notified the police, of course?' said Paul, but to his surprise she shook her head.

'No, I haven't,' she muttered, and there was an expression of uneasiness on her heavy face. 'I don't want the police messing about in my affairs. That's why I've come to you.'

'But surely, Mrs. Kilroe,' he protested, 'the police would be able to deal with this matter much better than I should. If your husband has met with an accident, or lost his memory, they would in all probability be able to tell you at once.'

She shifted uncomfortably in her chair. 'That's as may be, but I'd rather they weren't mixed up in it.'

A slight frown gathered on Paul Rivington's face. Obviously this woman had some very strong reason for distrusting the police. The most natural proceeding, in the circumstances she had described, would have been to inform the local police station. She hadn't done this. She had preferred to wait for three days and then to come to him. He felt very much inclined to refuse to have anything to do with the matter at all. It was only the fact that her name was Kilroe that prevented him from doing so. As he had said, the name was an uncommon one, and he still wondered if there could be any connection between this woman and her missing husband and the crotchety invalid at Datchet who called himself Coyne. He was another who had been chary of consulting the police. It was queer.

'I still think your best course would be to put the matter in the hands of the police,' he said, breaking the rather awkward silence. 'But since you seem disinclined to do that, perhaps you'll give me some more details.' He sat down at his desk and pulled a writing pad towards him. 'Where do you live, Mrs. Kilroe?'

'No. 17, Hatfield Terrace, Golder's Green,' she replied.

He noted the address and continued his questions. 'What time was it when your husband went out to post this letter?'

'About half past ten.'

'And you haven't seen him since?'

'No. I waited and waited, but he didn't come back. I thought at first he'd gone out for a bit of a walk, like he sometimes did, but when twelve o'clock come and there was no sign of him, I began to get worried.'

'What did you do then?'

'I didn't do nothing,' she answered. Almost unconsciously, she had pulled off her gloves, and Paul noticed that her fat hands were covered with rings. Obviously there was no lack of money in the Kilroe establishment.

'Do you mean,' he said incredulously, 'that you didn't take any steps or make any effort to find out what had happened to your husband?'

'What could I do,' she muttered, 'except go to the police? And I wasn't going to them. I wasn't sure — ' She stopped abruptly and bit her lip.

'You weren't sure of what?' he prompted. 'Go on, Mrs. Kilroe.'

'I wasn't sure,' she continued hesitantly, 'whether my husband 'ud like it.'

'What exactly do you mean by that?'

'Well . . . ' Her fingers plucked nervously at the fur on her coat. 'I . . . I suppose it ain't no use beating about the bush.' She returned his gaze defiantly. 'You see, my husband had been inside, and I didn't know but what he might not have gone of his own accord.'

'I see,' Paul said. Here was an explanation for her reluctance to have anything to do with the police.

'I don't want you to get it into your head, mister,' she continued rapidly, 'that my husband was a crook. He wasn't! But the police always had a grudge against him. They was always trying to pull something on him, and I wasn't sure but what he mightn't have gone for reasons of his own. Though I'm sure if he had, he'd have dropped me a line and let me know.'

'What was your husband's business?'

'He was a commission agent,' she said, and he concealed a smile. The designation 'commission agent' might mean anything. It was a business that could conceal a multitude of undertakings, honest or otherwise.

'He had an office, I presume?' he asked.

She nodded. 'Yes, only a small place, just off Holborn. He didn't go there much. He did most of his business from home. He ain't been near the office,' she added. 'I been down there each day.'

'Where was the office address?'

'Crane Buildings, Hack Street,' she answered, and Paul wrote it down, pursing his lips. He knew Hack Street very well. It was little more than an alley, not the sort of place where a man making sufficient money to supply his wife with jewellery of the kind Mrs. Kilroe wore would be likely to have business premises. It didn't require a great deal of intelligence to conclude that the source of Mr. Kilroe's wealth was not above suspicion. Apparently Mrs. Kilroe saw by his expression that the address of her husband's office hadn't impressed him, for she hastened to forestall any criticism he might make, and in doing so supplied him with all he wanted to know concerning the business activities of the missing man.

'You see, he didn't really want an office at all,' she explained hastily. 'Most of his deals was done over luncheon at different places. He used to buy things and sell 'em again, and made his profit on the difference.'

Paul nodded without comment. This sidelight on the methods of the missing Mr. Kilroe was most illuminating. Put more bluntly, he was a fence, a very profitable means of livelihood if judiciously and carefully carried out. There was no need to wonder anymore where the money came from that enabled his wife to smother her ugly hands in diamond rings and wrap her stout body in expensive furs; no need to feel any surprise that this hard-faced woman had been fearful of consulting the police.

'Had you any reason to suppose,' he asked, 'that this was going to happen? Did your husband drop any hint or in any way suggest that he might be going away suddenly?'

'No,' she answered. 'If he had, I shouldn't have been so worried.'

'Has he ever absented himself before, without letting you know his whereabouts?'

'No. Besides, if he'd known he wasn't coming back, he wouldn't have gone in his slippers.'

'Oh, he went in his slippers, did he?' murmured Paul in surprise. 'That certainly looks as if he'd had every intention of coming back. Was he in the habit of posting his own letters?' he said after a pause.

'Well, yes, now and again,' she replied, and there was a touch of embarrassment in her voice which for the moment he failed to understand; and then it dawned on him. Naturally, Mr. Kilroe would have correspondence with people whose addresses he might feel shy of exposing to the curious eye of others.

'It certainly seems rather strange,' he remarked, 'and I don't see how I'm going to be of much use to you. Supposing your husband to be absenting himself for reasons of his own, is there anywhere you can think of where he may have gone? Any relations — ' He stopped and looked at her enquiringly.

'My husband had no relations,' she said. 'He had several friends, but I been on the telephone to them and none of them's seen anything of him.'

Evidently, thought Paul, if she was speaking the truth, there was no connection between the man whom Mr. Weepers had addressed as Kilroe and the husband of this woman before him. It was curious, all the same. A most extraordinary coincidence. Not by any means unusual, for coincidences of that description were of the commonest occurrence in real life.

Everything went in twos, he had experienced that before. If you came upon an unusual name in the morning newspaper you almost invariably heard it again before the day was out. Still, it was queer all the same that he and Bob should have been discussing a man called Kilroe almost at the same time that this woman had chosen to make her call.

He found himself in something of a quandary. Beneath the harsh and forbidding exterior of Mrs. Kilroe, he could see that she was genuinely distressed, but he could do little to alleviate her anxiety. He saw small hope, even if he agreed to look into this matter of her husband's disappearance, of achieving any result. It was essentially a case for the police, with their wider facilities. A matter for organisation and routine rather than the subtler methods of analysis and deduction.

It was true there was a certain element of queerness about it. It was unusual for a man to disappear completely in the act of posting a letter, but Paul thought it was probably capable of a simple explanation. There was one in particular that had occurred to him, but which he was loath to put into words — the possibility that Mr. Kilroe's sudden disappearance might be traced to another woman. Such things are everyday occurrences, though Kilroe's method was certainly original.

'I really don't know what I can do,

Mrs. Kilroe,' he said, breaking the long silence. 'The information you've given me is so vague. You admit yourself that there's a distinct possibility that your husband may be absenting himself for reasons of his own.'

'I don't think that it's at all likely,' she said, 'but there's just a chance he may be, and I don't want to do anything that's going to put him in an awkward position, if you know what I mean.'

'Exactly!' He nodded. 'And therefore it rather ties our hands. I've already given you what I consider to be the best advice.'

Her mouth set stubbornly. Then: 'I'm not going to the police!' she declared. 'Anyway, not till I'm certain that James ain't gone on some business or other.'

She was so obviously torn between anxiety and loyalty to her husband that Paul felt a certain amount of sympathy for her. He realised what a difficult position she was in. She was aware that her husband's business was not strictly open and aboveboard, and was afraid of starting a hue and cry that might possibly annoy him, if it did nothing worse.

'You see how difficult it's?' he said. 'I can institute certain enquiries, it's true, but I haven't facilities for a worldwide search. For all we know, Mr. Kilroe may not be in England.'

'I'll be satisfied if you'd do what you can,' she said. 'And so far as expense is concerned, mister, I don't mind how much it costs — '

'It isn't a question of cost,' broke in Paul. 'We can discuss that later. I'll do what I can, Mrs. Kilroe, but I warn you beforehand that I don't think I shall be very successful. The first thing I shall want is a list of your husband's intimate friends and as many of his business acquaintances as you can give me.'

She complied with his request eagerly, but the information she had to offer was of the slenderest. Apparently James Kilroe had kept his affairs very much to himself.

Paul made notes of her replies, and, when he had exhausted this subject, enquired if she could supply him with a description of the missing man. 'I can do more than that,' she answered. 'I can give you a photograph. I thought you might want something of the sort, so I brought it along with me.' She opened the large crocodile-skin bag that rested on her lap and took out an oblong envelope. 'It's a good likeness,' she said, passing it across to the detective, 'although it was taken over five years ago. James hasn't altered much, though, except that he's got a little fatter.'

He opened the flap and drew out a cabinet portrait. The photograph was that of a middle-aged, well-preserved man, inclined to stoutness. The thick-lipped mouth was smiling, a smile that was not reflected in the rather hard eyes. The thick grey hair was brushed back over the round head, lending a spurious breadth to the rather low forehead.

Paul Rivington surveyed the heavy features with a curious sense of familiarity. Somewhere or at some time, he had seen or met Mr. James Kilroe, but he couldn't recollect where or in what circumstances. And then suddenly he realised.

With a quick movement, he covered the thick mass of hair with his thumb and knew that he hadn't been mistaken. The face in the photograph now was the face of the unknown man he had seen lying dead at the side of Spaniards Road!

10

A Consultation and a Discovery

There was no doubt; he was not misled by a chance resemblance. This photograph he held in his hand was without question that of the man whose body lay awaiting identification at the Hampstead Mortuary.

Rapidly he considered the situation. Should he tell the woman who sat watching him that her husband was dead, or should he postpone breaking the news until after he had had a consultation with Round Robin? She would have to know eventually, of course — it would be necessary for her to identify the body — but no particular purpose would be served by telling her now. There was always the faint possibility that he was mistaken, and it was as well to make definitely sure before committing himself.

'If you'll leave this with me, Mrs.

Kilroe,' he said, 'and give me your telephone number, I'll communicate with you as soon as I'm in possession of any news.'

She gave him the number, and he scribbled it below the other particulars he had taken.

'I'm very much obliged to you, mister,' she said, rising to her feet and wrapping her coat about her ample form. 'It's a relief to my mind to know that something's being done. Of course, if I hear from James in the meanwhile, I'll let you know.'

'Thank you,' said Paul, and he escorted her to the door. He was pretty certain in his own mind that she would never hear from James Kilroe again.

When he came back to the study after she'd gone, he found Bob gazing curiously at the photograph. 'What do you make of it?' he asked as Paul closed the door. 'Seems a queer business, doesn't it? Do you think there's any connection between this fellow and Coyne?'

'I don't think it, I'm sure of it!'

answered his brother. 'That's if the shock that brought on Coyne's fit was inspired by that newspaper paragraph.'

'What's that got to do with this fellow?' asked Bob in surprise.

'Everything! Unless I'm greatly mistaken, James Kilroe and the man who was found dead at Hampstead are one and the same.'

'So *that's* why you looked so peculiar when you saw the photograph,' Bob muttered.

'I'm not aware that I looked peculiar, but if I did, that's why.' He picked up the telephone and gave a number. 'Hello!' he said after a short interval. 'Put me through to Inspector Robin, will you?' There was a pause, and then: 'That you, Robin? Can you come round? I think I've got some interesting news for you . . . Yes, it's about the Hampstead business. I'm rather under the impression that I've succeeded in identifying the dead man.' He put the receiver back on its rest and sat down at his desk.

'It's a nice little problem,' he said musingly. 'Let's go over it and see how the pieces fit. Samuel Coyne, too crippled with rheumatism to come himself, sends his ward to request my assistance because three attempts have been made on his life and he fears a fourth. He denies all knowledge of these attacks insofar as the motive's concerned or who's responsible for them. This statement is obviously untrue, since he's taken the most elaborate precautions to prevent any unauthorised person getting into his house or grounds. His proposition to me is to act in the capacity of a bodyguard in case this fourth attempt, which he fears, should be made. I refuse to accept the commission, but arrange for you to go down, since I'm rather interested in the situation.

'On the night that you go down to Datchet, I'm driving home and am present at the discovery of a dead man on the side of Spaniards Road at Hampstead; a dead man from whose body every means of identification has been removed and whose head has been completely shaved. It's evidently a case of murder, and the crime has just as obviously not been committed at the place where the body is found. The victim was killed somewhere else and transported to Spaniards Road by car. The clothing is that of a tramp, but the condition of the body shows that the dead man was well nourished and cared for. While the police are investigating the crime, you, at Datchet, are alarmed during the night by an attempt to break into Coyne's house. You catch the intruder, who turns out to be a fifth-rate burglar, well known to the police by the name of Alf Weepers. This man recognises Coyne as somebody who he calls Kilroe. Coyne is so scared at the recognition that he lets the man go, concocting some cock-and-bull story about not wishing to prosecute.

'Later it's discovered that Coyne's — or Kilroe's — ward, Diana Fielding, has disappeared under peculiar circumstances. She's apparently decided to run away during the night, and has been assisted in this by some unknown person in a car.

'A brief account of the Hampstead murder appears in the *Megaphone*, owing to the accidental presence of a reporter on the staff of that newspaper at the police station when the crime was reported. Samuel Coyne, or Kilroe, reads the account and promptly throws a fit. The description of the dead man in the paper is so vague that he couldn't possibly have recognised him.

'You come up to acquaint me with the night's happenings at Datchet, and are here when a woman named Mrs. Kilroe arrives for the purpose of asking me to find her husband, who has disappeared after going out ostensibly to post a letter. She's reluctant to inform the police because the husband is engaged in shady dealings; in fact, frankly, he's a fence. To assist me in investigating his disappearance, she supplies a photograph that turns out to be of the unknown man found dead at the side of Spaniards Road. That's the whole thing in a nutshell.'

'And it doesn't make sense!' growled Bob.

'On the contrary, it does; but there are gaps.'

'Caverns would be a better description,' said Bob, frowning.

'Well, caverns, if you like,' said Paul amiably. 'There's no doubt that all these incidents are connected. The first thing I asked Coyne was whether he'd informed the police about these attempts made on his life. He hadn't! He offered the excuse — a very lame one — that he did not wish the matter to become public property. When I advised Mrs. Kilroe to go to the police, she answered in very much the same strain, although she was a little more candid about it. Now, the question is: who murdered Kilroe, and is he the same person who's attempted to kill Coyne three times?'

'There's more than one question,' said Bob. 'There's half a dozen and more. Why did the man who killed Kilroe shave off all his hair? Why did that fact upset Coyne when he read of it to such an extent that he fainted from fright? What connection is there between Coyne, whose real name is Kilroe, and the other Kilroe who was murdered? So far as I can see, they must be some sort of relations.

It's impossible that the name could be a coincidence.'

Paul nodded. 'Any more questions?'

'Yes. Where is Miss Diana Fielding, and what made her leave the house so hurriedly? What is it that Weepers knows about Coyne that made him so anxious to let him go? Why — '

'I think that'll do for the moment,' interrupted his brother, smiling wryly. 'I hope you don't expect me to answer all these offhand, because I can't. It's as much a puzzle to me as it's to you, but it's a very interesting puzzle all the same. One thing should be fairly easy: to find out what Weepers knows. I don't suppose it'll be difficult to discover his whereabouts, and even less difficult to make him talk. The answers to your other questions will doubtless come to light in their proper sequence. Did you tell Coyne that you were coming to see me?'

'Yes, and he seemed rather reluctant that I should go.'

'I think it'd be a good idea,' remarked Paul thoughtfully, 'if you got back to Datchet as soon as possible. We don't want anything to happen during your absence.'

'What d'you think's likely to happen? I shouldn't think Coyne's mysterious enemy would risk an attempt in broad daylight.'

'I'm not considering that possibility,' said Paul, shaking his head, 'so much so that while you're away, something might happen that would be useful for us to know. We know so little at the moment that the smallest detail we can add to our knowledge is bound to be of help. I've got a pretty shrewd idea that the hub of the whole mystery is to be found at Datchet.'

'Why do you think that?'

'I don't know that I can explain,' Paul said with a shrug. 'You can call it a hunch or instinct. It's pretty obvious, however, from what we know, that Coyne's aware of the reason why this unfortunate man Kilroe's head was shaved. If he didn't know, the mention of the finding of a dead man with his head shaved wouldn't have upset him. And if he knows that, he knows everything, for I'm convinced that that's the key to the whole business.'

'We're not definitely certain, though, that it was that paragraph in the paper that sent him into a faint.'

'It's very difficult to be certain of anything,' remarked Paul a little tritely, leaning back in his chair. 'One can only follow the law of probability. The paper was open at that particular page. There was nothing else on it, you say, which could have been remotely responsible for a shock such as Coyne must have suffered. Add to this the fact that with the exception of the servant, Gunter; that he was alone at the time; and that his real name is the same as that of the murdered man, and I don't think there can be much doubt.' He stopped as there came a sharp knocking from below. 'That's Robin,' he said, and a few moments later the fat inspector, red-faced and breathless, burst into the room.

'What's all this, Mr. Rivington?' he panted, throwing his hat into a chair. 'You discovered the identity of that fellow?'

'I think so,' said Paul. 'Take a look at that!' He pushed the photograph of Mrs. Kilroe's husband across the desk, and

Round Robin bent over it. 'Cover up the hair,' suggested Paul, 'and you'll see.'

The inspector did so and uttered an exclamation. 'This is the man all right,' he said. 'How did you get hold of it? Who is he?'

'The name is James Kilroe, or rather it was,' said the detective. 'And the photograph was given me by his wife a few minutes ago.' He explained as shortly as possible the interview he had had with the woman, and Mr. Robin listened, his forehead wrinkled in a frown.

'Queer business,' he commented. 'Went out to post a letter and wasn't seen again until his body was discovered at the side of Spaniards Road.'

'He was seen by somebody,' corrected Paul, 'and that was the person who killed him.'

'Do you think he was a fence?'

'He was obviously a crook of some sort. It was because his wife knew this that she didn't communicate with the police.'

'He's never been through our hands.'

'Oh, yes he has. I don't know how long

ago, but his wife let that out. He served a sentence for something or other.'

'In that case, they'll have his finger-prints in records. That'll clinch the identification of the body.'

'Yes, that's peculiar. I hadn't thought of that.' Paul frowned.

'Hadn't thought of what?'

'Didn't you send his fingerprints to records for possible identification?'

'Yes, but we've had no report from them yet,' replied Mr. Robin. 'Can you get hold of this woman? We'd better take her over to the mortuary as soon as possible and get her to identify the man.'

'She won't have had time to get home yet,' said Paul with a glance at the clock. 'I'll ring her up later this afternoon and arrange for us to be picked up at Hampstead.'

'It's an extraordinary business,' said Round Robin. 'It's that shaved head that gets me. Why was it done? Why, after killing the man, did his murderer want to shave all his hair off?'

'I can't suggest any reasonable theory,' confessed Paul, 'As you say, the thing's extraordinary. If this fellow was James Kilroe, he must have been picked up by his murderer either on his way to, or returning from, the pillar-box, and taken to the place where he was eventually killed. That was the night before his body was found, so for nearly twenty-four hours he was somewhere either dead or alive. It'd be interesting to discover where.'

'Might be anywhere,' said the inspector. 'The doctor said he'd been dead for a long time. He wasn't very definite as to how long, but he said certainly more than twelve hours. Well, anyway,' he added hopefully, 'we've got something to go on. We know who he was, and that's the most important end to a murder case. I expect when we begin enquiring into his past, we shall discover a motive for the crime.'

'I wonder if it's going to be as easy as that,' murmured Paul, thinking of the frightened man at Datchet of whom Mr. Robin was so far unaware. 'Do you know Alf Weepers?'

The stout inspector looked at him in surprise. 'Every policeman in the force

142

knows Weepers. He's been through our hands over and over again. Why?'

'Know where he lives?'

'No,' answered Mr. Robin. 'Not off-hand. What's the idea?'

'I wish you'd pull him in on some pretext or other. I'd like a word with him.'

'Why?' demanded the inspector, his bright eyes full of curiosity. 'What's he got to do with this business?'

'I don't know, but maybe a lot,' replied Paul. And then, before Mr. Robin could put the question he saw hovering on his lips, he added, 'Ever heard of a man called Samuel Coyne?'

'No!' The answer was a little irritable. 'What are you getting at? Who's Samuel Coyne?'

'He's a gentleman who lives at Datchet,' explained Paul, 'and — ' The telephone bell interrupted him with a shrill clamour, and stretching out his hand he picked up the receiver. 'Hello!' he said, and after a moment turned to Mr. Robin. 'It's the Yard. They want to speak to you.'

'Oh yes, I told them I'd be here in case

anything came through,' muttered the inspector, taking the telephone from Paul's hand. 'Robin speaking. What's that . . . ? At Wimbledon . . . ? All right, I'll go straight there.' He slammed the instrument back on its rest and turned a startled face towards Paul. 'The Wimbledon police have just notified me of the discovery of a body in one of the more secluded parts of the common,' he announced. 'The body of a man dressed in ragged clothes from which every mark of identification has been removed. And that's not all.' He paused, and looked at Paul queerly.

'Go on,' said Rivington, though he guessed what was coming.

'The man's head had been shaved!' finished the inspector, and there was incredulity in his voice and amazement in his small beady eyes.

11

The Second Crime

The little group stood among the thickly growing silver birches, gazing down at the thing that lay half-hidden in the wet bracken. The drizzle of rain which had been falling all the morning had ceased for a while, though the aspect of the sky, visible through the tracery of branches overhead, gave little promise of it being for long.

It was still and silent here in the heart of the common. On all sides stretched an endless vista of silvery-grey trunks, and the only sound was the uneven dripping from the rain-sodden branches onto the carpet of dead leaves and bracken. It was an eerie spot even in the full light of day, rendered more eerie by that still and silent figure which lay motionless, its face upturned to the sullen sky.

Mr. Robin gave a little shiver and

glanced at the divisional inspector who stood near him. 'This was exactly how he was found?' he enquired.

The man nodded. 'Yes, sir. Nothing has been touched. The divisional surgeon has made his examination, of course; but knowing you were on the way, we took care not to disturb the body.'

Paul Rivington, who had accompanied the Scotland Yard man, looked down at the dead man. The ragged clothes and collar-less shirt gave him the appearance of a tramp. A slight grey moustache shadowed the upper lip, and by some contraction of the muscles the mouth was set in the semblance of a sardonic grin, as though the dead man were regarding the affair as part of a huge joke. The head was bald, devoid of every vestige of hair; and on the gleaming skull was evidence of the hastily used razor that had achieved this result.

'Horrible, isn't it?' muttered Mr. Robin, his mouth set. Paul nodded without replying.

There was no need to look twice in order to discover the cause of death. The front of the ragged waistcoat was stiff with blood, and there was a narrow slit on the left side immediately over the heart. 'As in the other case, he's been stabbed,' Paul muttered. 'Has the body been searched?'

'Yes, sir,' said the local man, 'but the pockets had been cleared of everything. Nor are there any marks on the clothing.'

'It's a repetition of the other crime. The man wasn't killed here at all.'

'You think the body was brought here after the murder? Same as the other was?'

Paul nodded. 'I should say that both murders were committed at the same time.'

'Who are we dealing with?' The inspector frowned. 'A demented barber? What the dickens was the object of shaving these men's heads?'

'And removing everything by which they might be identified,' augmented Paul thoughtfully. 'I wonder who this poor fellow was.' He stooped over the body, peered at the hands, and glanced at the patch of chest that was visible through the open neck of the shirt. 'Not so well acquainted with the luxuries of life as the unfortunate Mr. Kilroe,' he remarked. 'This fellow has done a certain amount of manual labour, I should say, by the appearance of his hands. Who made the discovery?'

'A man named Mason, sir.' It was the divisional inspector who supplied the information. 'He was out for a walk with his dog. Although this is a pretty secluded part, it's not far from one of the main paths that cross the common, as you know. The animal ran in among the trees and wouldn't come out when he was whistled. Mr. Mason followed him to see why, and discovered the body. He notified the policeman on patrol, who reported the matter to the police station. We'd heard about the other affair at Hampstead and immediately phoned the Yard.'

'The next step is to find out who he was,' said Mr. Robin. 'I don't think you need leave him here any longer, eh, Mr. Rivington?'

Paul shook his head, and at a signal from the divisional inspector, two uniformed constables who had been waiting for that purpose picked up the dead man and carried him to the wheeled ambulance at the side of the main path.

Paul made a search of the place where the body had lain, but found nothing. There were no marks of blood on the crushed bracken, and he pointed this out to Mr. Robin. 'It's further evidence he wasn't killed here,' he said. 'The wound bled copiously, and there would have been traces of blood near the body.'

'Two exactly similar crimes,' muttered the inspector. 'What's at the back of it, Mr. Rivington?'

'Something very big,' replied Paul gravely 'I said that when the first murder was discovered, and I'm more sure of it than ever now.'

'But what?'

'We shall know that, when we discover why these two men's heads were shaved. That's obviously the key to the whole mystery.'

'I've been wondering,' said the inspector thoughtfully, 'whether it may not have been done just to make us think that — a sort of blind to lead us away from the real motive.'

'I should be inclined to agree with you but for one thing. You remember my asking you if you'd ever heard of a man called Samuel Coyne, before the telephone message came through?'

'Yes.' The inspector looked at him keenly. 'What do you mean?'

'Wait till we get back to the car, and I'll tell you.'

The divisional inspector and the sergeant who was with him had gone on ahead. As they came out at the place where Paul had left his car, they saw them standing by the side of a small machine that had brought them from the station.

'Just let me have a word with Rawson,' said Mr. Robin, 'and I'll come back.'

He went over to the local man while Paul got into his car and started the engine. The police car, containing the inspector and his subordinates, moved off as Mr. Robin rejoined him.

'Where do you want to go?' asked Paul as the other got in beside him. 'The station?'

The inspector shook his head. 'Not unless you do. There's nothing further I can do there at the moment. The next step is to put in motion routine enquiries concerning the fellow's identity. What's this you're going to tell me?'

Paul waited until he had turned the car and was heading towards the main thoroughfare; and then, as briefly as possible, he recounted to his companion the story of the frightened man at Datchet. Round Robin listened interestedly, his brows drawn together.

'Rum sort of business,' he remarked when Paul had finished. 'If this fellow Coyne's real name is Kilroe, it looks as though there might be a connection.'

'I'm pretty certain there is,' said his friend decisively. 'Though what it is, I'll admit I haven't the least idea. It's too much to suggest that the similarity of names is a coincidence, particularly when taken in conjunction with the effect that newspaper report had on the man.'

'Yes,' said the inspector, pursing his lips. 'I think I ought to see this fellow, Mr.

Rivington, and try and get something out of him.'

'It would be a very unwise move, in my opinion. I doubt if it'd do any good, and it might do a considerable amount of harm. You couldn't force Coyne to speak, and you've nothing against him. He evidently isn't responsible for the murders. The man's unable to walk, and apart from that will probably be able to produce evidence that he was at the house at Datchet at the time these men were killed. If you question him, all you'll do will be to put him on his guard. At the present moment, he can't suspect that we've any idea there's a link between himself and these two dead men.'

The other agreed, but reluctantly. 'I see your point. But at the same time, if the man knows anything, he ought to be made to disclose it. What's at the bottom of all these precautions? Who's he afraid of?'

'Presumably, the person responsible for these murders. That seems to be the most obvious conclusion.'

'Hm!' said the inspector dubiously.

'Well, something ought to be done about him.'

'Something *is* being done about him,' said Paul, turning the car into the main road. 'Bob's gone back there now, and we can depend upon him to keep a sharp lookout for anything that may be of importance. He's aware that Coyne may be mixed up in this other business, and will be doubly watchful.'

'I wonder what happened to the ward,' mused the inspector. 'That seems a bit queer.'

'It seems to me very queer,' answered Paul, and there was a grave note in his voice. 'I'm rather worried about her, Robin. The whole business of her disappearance strikes me as being peculiarly unsatisfactory.'

'Maybe she just got tired of this fellow's grumbling and legged it.'

'Perhaps,' agreed the other without a great deal of conviction. 'Well, now you know why I suggested you should pull in Alf Weepers. He knows something about Coyne, and if he'll talk, his knowledge might help us.'

'I'll have him in Cannon Row before nightfall!' declared Round Robin optimistically. 'You'd better telephone Mrs. Kilroe when we get back. She'll have to come along to Hampstead and identify her husband.'

'We might get her to look at the other body, too. It's quite possible she might know the man.'

Mrs. Kilroe came to Hampstead in response to the message; an agitated and tearful woman, for Paul had broken the news as gently as possible over the wire, considering that it was best to prepare her as far in advance as possible for her ordeal. They drove to the mortuary, and after certain preliminaries were admitted to the cold, gloomy apartment where, under the light of an unshaded electric bulb, the man whose body had been discovered at the side of Spaniards Road lay upon a stone slab.

Mrs. Kilroe gave one look at the prone figure, and with a choked scream fainted. They took her into the office of the official in charge, and when she recovered she left no doubt as to the identity of the dead man.

'It's James,' she wailed through her tears. 'Oh my God, who could have done it? Who could have done it?'

There was no contesting the genuineness of her emotion, and Paul pacified her as best he could. 'I'm afraid, Mrs. Kilroe,' he said gently, 'we shall have to ask you to perform a further unpleasant task.' He explained what was wanted of her, but she shook her head violently.

'I'll not go!' she said. 'This has been such a shock to me that I don't feel capable of undergoing another.'

'You wish to see the person responsible for your husband's death punished, I suppose?'

Her eyes hardened and her mouth set. 'If I knew who it was, I'd kill him myself,' she answered viciously.

'Well, then, try and make an effort and do what we ask,' he urged. 'If this man should prove to be known to you, it's going to help the police considerably; and the longer his identification is delayed, the more chance it gives for the murderer to get away.'

His argument proved successful. Mrs. Kilroe set her lips. 'Very well, I'll go,' she said, and they escorted her out to the waiting car.

But the identity of the other victim was not to be discovered so easily; for, to Paul's chagrin, Mrs. Kilroe showed no sign of recognition when she was shown the body.

'I've never seen him before in my life!' she declared. 'He's a complete stranger to me, mister.'

Both Paul and the inspector were disappointed. But she was obviously speaking the truth, and there was nothing more to be said.

'Did your husband ever mention a man named Samuel Coyne?' asked the detective as they drove back to Hampstead.

'No, I can't recollect the name,' she said. 'He may have known a man called that, but he never mentioned it to me.'

They put her in a taxi when they reached the house and sent her home, no longer tearful but dry-eyed and hard-faced, although beneath that stony surface Paul detected a very genuine grief.

'Well, we've discovered who one of the dead men was,' said Mr. Robin, 'and that's something.'

His tone implied that it was not much, and Paul was forced to agree with him. It opened up a fresh line of enquiry, however, which might quite possibly yield results. An inspection into James Kilroe's past could perhaps supply a clue not only to the reason for his death but what connection there was, if any, between himself and the terrified Samuel Coyne.

Paul remarked on this to Mr. Robin, and the inspector nodded. 'It's the obvious thing to do, of course,' he said. 'I'll be getting back to the Yard and start those enquiries going.'

'Let me know as soon as you get hold of Weepers,' said Paul as the inspector took his leave. 'I'm rather interested to hear what he has to say.'

He would have been more interested still had he known the contents of a certain letter, laboriously penned, which Mr. Weepers had that morning slipped into a pillar-box in the region of Westminster Bridge Road, and which was addressed to the man who called himself Samuel Coyne.

12

Mr. Weepers is Obstinate

Mr. Weepers was in high spirits as he emerged from the gloomy house in Lambeth in which that morning he had rented a room. The narrow evil-smelling street was familiar to him, for he had lived here during most of the time he hadn't spent in prison. Mrs. Glott had welcomed him with the solicitude of an old friend; a solicitude which had become even more marked when Mr. Weepers had produced a roll of notes from the pocket of his shabby trousers and laid a month's rent in advance.

'Been away for a little holiday, I suppose?' she said, thus tactfully suggesting that her lodger's absence had been caused by close contact with the interior of one of His Majesty's prisons.

'No,' said Mr. Weepers. 'Been 'avin' a run of bad luck lately and 'ad ter doss where they don't charge you nothin'. Life's full of ups and downs, and last night I struck one of the ups, an' 'ere I am.'

'You can 'ave your old room,' said the landlady condescendingly, making no effort to enquire too closely into the 'up' Mr. Weepers had referred to. 'And if you'd like anythin' to eat, just say so.'

Mr. Weepers said so, and was provided with a large plate of eggs and bacon flanked by a pot of tea which made up in quantity what it lacked in quality. When he had satisfied his hunger, he lit a cigarette from the packet which Mrs. Glott's grimy offspring had fetched for him, and settling himself in a knobbly armchair, trickled smoke through his nostrils and thought over his good fortune.

He had spoken no more than the truth when he had told the landlady that he had been up against it. Life for Mr. Weepers during the last few weeks had been very hard indeed. He had spent the greater part of it on the road, almost penniless, and sleeping wherever he could

160

find a likely-looking place to stretch his weary bones. And then had come that amazing stroke of luck which had almost in a flash altered his entire prospects.

He had been practically at the end of his tether when he had made his attempt to break into The Wilderness, and now, in comparison to his previous position, he was on velvet. What a bit of luck, choosing old Kilroe's house! He was still congratulating himself as he came out of the ill-lighted street into the more populated thoroughfare of Kennington Road and turned his steps westwards.

Chance had put him onto a good thing, and although his clothes were shabby and his boots down at heel, he walked jauntily. In his pocket was the greater part of the twenty pounds the tenant of The Wilderness had parted with in return for his silence. And it was only the first instalment. Kilroe didn't know that, but Weepers did. He foresaw visions of easy and regular money, and the prospect was a very pleasant one. He had already written suggesting a further appointment so that this idea of his could be put on a proper business footing.

In the meanwhile, after his long abstinence, he decided to spend the evening in celebrating his good fortune. There was a certain pub in a street of Shaftesbury Avenue where Mr. Weepers's unprepossessing face had been quite well-known in the days of his affluence, and where he would be certain to meet a number of cronies who, provided he was well supplied with money, would welcome him with open arms. It would, he decided, be an evening of unlimited beer and hilarity.

He boarded a passing bus and was set down at Cambridge Circus. His appearance in the bar of the public house which had been his objective was greeted with surprise and a certain amount of misgiving. The misgivings remained until Mr. Weepers produced a pound note and ordered himself a pint of bitter.

'Wot you been up to, Alf?' enquired a little man, coming over to his side as he scooped up his change.

'Been 'avin' a rest for a few weeks,' answered Mr. Weepers loftily as he took a long drink from the foaming glass which was pushed across the counter towards him.

'Been in bird, eh?' asked a stout jovial-faced man who made a comfortable if precarious living flying the kite for a gang of cheque stealers.

'No, I ain't!' said Mr. Weepers with dignity. 'If you must know, I've been on the floor, but I'm in the market again now.' Thus in the slang of the underworld he intimated briefly that he had been hard up but was doing well again.

'Wot was the lay, Alf?' asked the man, who worked as cover to a pickpocket. 'Done a bust?'

'Yeah,' said Mr. Weepers, finishing his beer. 'Wot'll you 'ave, boys?'

He supplied their various suggestions, and settled down with the vanity of the habitual criminal to offer a totally imaginative account of how he had come by his newfound wealth. The truth he rigidly suppressed, knowing full well that the man who put the black on another was looked askance upon.

He was in the middle of his seventh

beer, and his eyes in consequence had assumed a slightly glassy appearance, when the buzz of conversation around him suddenly ceased, and he felt a touch on his arm. Looking round quickly, he saw a big man standing at his elbow.

'Havin' a good time, Weepers?' said the newcomer.

'Supposin' I am, wot's it got to do with you?' demanded Mr. Weepers, recognising in the man beside him a natural enemy. 'Can't a feller spend an evenin' with 'is friends without interference from you bogies?'

Sergeant Halter smiled good-humouredly. 'Sorry to interrupt you, Weepers,' he said, 'but I want you to come for a little walk with me.'

Mr. Weepers's small eyes snapped dangerously. 'Wot's the idea?' he demanded, full of the courage which the beer had instilled in him. 'You ain't got nothin' on me. Leave me alone!'

'Don't be silly,' said the detective. 'You don't want to make any trouble. Of course I've got nothing on you, but they want to have a little chat with you at the

Yard. Finish your drink and come along.'

'Likely, ain't it!' Mr. Weepers was scornful. 'You just says come along, and I follers like a ruddy lamb — I don't think!'

'None of you fellows think!' retorted Halter. 'If you had enough brains to know when to come in out of the rain, you wouldn't be crooks. Drink your beer and come along. I'm being friendly now, but if you make a fuss I'll show you just how nasty I can be.'

'Wot's the charge?' demanded Mr. Weepers indignantly.

'I've told you,' said the sergeant wearily, 'there isn't any charge. We just want to have a talk with you, that's all.'

'I see,' said the burglar sarcastically. 'Feelin' a bit dull and lonely and want me to come and cheer things up. Wot's the gag?' In spite of his attitude, he was inwardly alarmed at this unexpected interruption to his evening's amusement.

'That's it,' said the smiling Halter. 'The commissioner's giving a party and he wants you to entertain the guests.'

Mr. Weepers decided that discretion was the better part of valour. 'All right,

165

I'll come.' And with a word to his late companions, he accompanied the broad-shouldered sergeant through the swing doors into the street.

On the way to the Yard, he tried to discover the reason for this urgent need of his presence, but the detective was not in a confidential mood.

'You'll see when you get there, my lad,' he said in answer to Mr. Weepers's questions. 'And if you behave yourself and do as you're told, there'll be no trouble coming to you.'

The burglar was not so sure of this. When they got down from the bus at the corner of Whitehall and passed under the arch leading to police headquarters, he was full of misgivings. He was taken up to a waiting-room, thrust into the bare, cheerless apartment, and left there in charge of a plainclothes constable. He attempted to cross-examine this man, but the constable was as reticent as the sergeant, declaring frankly that he hadn't the least idea why Mr. Weepers had been brought there. Which was the truth, although Mr. Weepers, with that ingrained suspicion which was one of the characteristics of his class, steadfastly believed he was lying.

He was kept waiting for nearly three quarters of an hour, and then Sergeant Halter came back and took him up two flights of stairs, eventually ushering him into a room almost as bare and cheerless as the waiting-room, but furnished with a desk behind which sat a familiar figure.

'Come in, Weepers,' said Mr. Robin. 'Sit down over there.'

Mr. Weepers perched himself on the edge of the chair he had indicated. 'Wot's the meaning of this?' he demanded. 'Wot right 'ave you to take a man away from 'is friends — ' He broke off as his roving eyes lighted on the other man who was present. 'Blimey!' he exclaimed. 'Rivington! So you're in this too, are yer? Wot's the game?'

'There's no game, Weepers,' said Mr. Robin. 'We want to ask you one or two questions, that's all.'

Mr. Weepers sniffed. 'That's all you bloomin' busies ever do,' he said disparagingly. 'Go about askin' questions till you get some poor bloke to convict 'imself!'

'We've no wish for you to convict yourself,' put in Paul quietly. 'But we're under the impression that you have information which may be of value to us in the investigation of a murder case.'

The man's small eyes opened wide. 'I don't know nothin' about no murder!' he said hastily. 'Wot you tryin' to pull on me?'

'Nothing at all!' said Mr. Robin impatiently. 'If we were going to pull anything on you, d'you think we'd waste our time having you up here? You were at Datchet in the early hours of this morning, weren't you?'

Mr. Weepers considered. It was his settled policy never to answer a question straightforwardly. The fact that Paul Rivington was present, however, and that his brother had been the person who had caught him in his attempt to break into The Wilderness, forced him for once to break his rule.

'Supposin' I was,' he answered. 'There weren't nothin' in it. I explained to the gentleman that I was lookin' for some-where to kip — '

'We're not trying to prove a charge against you,' broke in Paul.

'You couldn't if you wanted to!' said Mr. Weepers triumphantly. 'You might get me for bein' on enclosed premises with intent, but that's all you could do. I knows the law!'

'We all know the law,' snapped Mr. Robin, beginning to get irritable. 'Now listen, Weepers. You know something about a man named Samuel Coyne, the tenant of the house where you were looking for somewhere to kip.'

'I know somethin' about him?' Mr. Weepers's face was the picture of surprised innocence. 'I don't know nothin' about 'im — except that 'e's a gentleman.'

'According to my brother,' said Paul, 'on first seeing him, you recognised him and addressed him as Kilroe.'

'Me?' exclaimed Mr. Weepers. 'If I never move from this spot — '

'Cut out all that stuff!' said Mr. Robin. 'You recognised this man and called him

169

Kilroe. Now what do you know about him?'

'I told you,' said the man with dignity. 'I don't know nothin'!'

'Then why did you call him Kilroe?' asked Paul. 'It's no good denying it, because my brother heard you distinctly.'

''E must 'ave imagined.it!' declared Mr. Weepers. 'Why should I call him Kilroe when 'is name's Coyne?'

'That's what we want to know,' said Round Robin.

'And if I could tell yer I would,' said Mr. Weepers frankly. 'There's nothin' I wouldn't do to 'elp the perlice. A fine body of men, as I've always said — '

'Yes, yes, I've no doubt you have,' said Paul, concealing a smile. 'But let's stick to the point. You recognised Coyne as someone you'd known as Kilroe. He knew you'd recognised him, and to keep your mouth shut he refused to prefer a charge against you.'

'You got it all wrong. I don't know no one of the name of Kilroe. And as fer this feller Coyne — and a finer gentleman never lived — 'e was sorry fer me, that's

170

all. 'E knew I didn't look the sort of person wot 'ud commit a burglary. I explained to 'im that I was only lookin' fer a shed to doss down in, and 'e believed me.'

'I'll bet he did!' said the sceptical Mr. Robin. 'Are you sticking to that story, Weepers?'

'Can a man do more than tell the truth? You wouldn't 'ave me tell a lie, would yer?'

'Then your story is,' put in Paul, 'that my brother was mistaken, that you didn't address Mr. Coyne as Kilroe, and he let you go because he was sorry for you? Is that it?'

'That's it! I couldn't 'ave put it better meself.'

'Then,' snapped the detective, 'how is it that last night you were looking for somewhere to sleep because you hadn't got the money to pay for a bed, and this evening Sergeant Halter finds you in a pub in Shaftesbury Avenue buying drinks for all your friends? Where did you get the money from?'

For an instant, Mr. Weepers was

171

confused. 'I — I met a man this morning,' he answered after a pause, 'wot 'ad owed me some money for a long time, an' 'e paid me.'

Paul looked across at Mr. Robin, and the inspector shrugged his shoulders.

'You're sure you didn't get this money from Coyne?' persisted Paul. 'Think well before you answer, Weepers, because this may be a serious business for you.'

Mr. Weepers shook his head. 'I didn't get no money from Coyne!' he stated emphatically. 'And you can't prove I did.'

Paul Rivington's lips compressed. He knew that. Provided the burglar stuck to his story, there was no proof. For a quarter of an hour, he and Mr. Robin between them tried to shake him, but Mr. Weepers was obstinate and in the end they gave up.

'You'd better let him go,' said Paul, and the burglar went, hastily and triumphantly.

'He was lying, of course,' said Paul when he had gone. 'But I don't think you'd have got anything out of him if you'd kept him here all night. It's my belief he's been well-paid to keep his mouth shut.'

'In which case he'll never talk,' growled Mr. Robin. 'I know these fellows, and you know 'em, too. They only squeal when it's to their advantage.'

'The best thing you can do is to put a man to tail him up. We may learn something that way.'

'I'll do that now,' said the inspector. He picked up the house telephone, called a number, and spoke rapidly. The result of his action was that when Mr. Weepers complacently left Scotland Yard, he was followed at a respectful distance by an unobtrusive man whose duty it was not to let him out of his sight.

Unfortunately for the success of this plan, Detective-Constable Ayling lost his quarry in the crowd occasioned by a street accident at the junction of Kennington Road and Fitzalan Street, a fact that was to bring upon him a severe reprimand from his superior, and prove even more unfortunate for the welfare of Mr. Weepers.

13

The Lurking Man

Bob arrived at The Wilderness in the dusk of the evening and was admitted by the sullen-faced Gunter. As the heavy prison-like gates closed behind him, he asked the servant if Samuel Coyne was better. 'He's all right,' was the surly reply. 'Blimey, what a barny! Fancy a grown man throwing a fit like that!' He accompanied Bob up the weed-grown drive and preceded him into the house.

Mr. Coyne occupied his usual place in front of the study fire. His face was drawn and haggard, and the fear in his eyes was more pronounced.

'I'm glad you've got back,' he said as Bob entered. 'It's rather dull here with only Gunter, and you know what he's like.'

Bob pulled up a chair. 'Are you feeling all right now?'

'Oh, yes, thank you,' said Coyne. 'These attacks never last very long.'

'You've had them before?'

'Twice. It's something to do with my heart. I'm afraid I gave you rather a bad scare.'

Bob waved aside the apology. Coyne's explanation for his fit, or whatever it was, did not deceive him for a moment. He was convinced that the attack hadn't been due to heart trouble, and was equally convinced that Coyne was not subject to such things. However, it was not policy to let the man become aware of his suspicions concerning the news paragraph, and therefore he changed the subject. 'Is there any news of Miss Fielding?' he asked.

Coyne's brows darkened. 'No, there isn't. I don't suppose there will be. She found life here too dull, I suppose, and cleared off. I was annoyed at the time because it was an ungrateful thing to do after all I've done for her. The least she could have done was to have told me she was going away. But there you are; that's usually what happens. You do things out of pure kindness and all you get in return is kicks.'

There had, Bob privately considered, been little kindness in Samuel Coyne's attitude towards his ward, but he kept his thoughts to himself. 'Is she related to you in any way?' he asked.

'No; I merely acted as her guardian. She's the daughter of — of an old friend of mine who died. She was eighteen at the time of his death, and I offered to look after her.'

He seemed curiously reluctant to discuss her, and began to talk desultorily about the weather and other more or less unimportant subjects. Bob saw that his mind was occupied with something of grave importance, for every now and again he wavered in what he was saying and seemed to find difficulty in picking up the threads.

He was in the midst of a rather uninteresting dissertation concerning his view of the government's foreign policy when Bob made the discovery that he had run out of cigarettes. He had intended to purchase a supply when he got out of the train at Datchet, but it had slipped his memory.

'I have plenty,' said Coyne, twisting in his chair towards the desk and reaching for the box he kept there.

But Bob declined his offer. Coyne smoked Turkish and he preferred the more common Virginia. 'I'll go down and get some before dinner,' he announced. 'There's plenty of time.'

His host suggested sending Gunter; but Bob, who was rather relieved at the prospect of getting away from the house and the companionship of Mr. Coyne which the excuse offered, would not entertain the idea. 'A walk will do me good,' he said, and he went out to find Gunter to open the gate for him.

The servant complied grumblingly, and Bob strode off towards the village thankfully. Although he was intensely interested in Samuel Coyne and the mystery that surrounded him, the task Paul had set him was not by any means an enviable one. The atmosphere of the house jarred on him. The undercurrent of fear that showed in everything Coyne did was irritating. The air of expectancy which seemed to lurk in every corner of the gloomy building was conducive to bringing about a restlessness that Bob found extremely unpleasant. He would have welcomed action in any form. It was this waiting that got on his nerves. It wouldn't have been so bad had Coyne's personality been different, but Bob disliked him intensely, and the prospect of remaining shut up in that prison-like dwelling with only Coyne and Gunter's companionship — the maid who came daily could scarcely be taken into account — was uninspiring in the extreme.

For the twentieth time, he wondered of what and of whom Samuel Coyne was afraid. What had the man done to arouse an enmity so great that three attempts should already have been made on his life? Bob was prepared to admit that he could imagine him capable of anything, but what was the true reason? That he credited the unknown person whom he feared with a tenacity beyond the average was evident the extraordinary precautions he had taken to guard his personal safety.

Was it the same hand that had struck down the other two men which he feared? The fact that the man who had been found at the side of Spaniards Road was named Kilroe was queer. Could he be a relation, and was his death the result of a feud against the whole family of Kilroes?

This was an idea that hadn't occurred to him before, and he considered it. There was that second crime to be accounted for, the news of which had reached Paul just before he left. Was it possible that the dead man who had been discovered at Wimbledon was also named Kilroe?

Bob thought he had hit on something. It was a possibility, and he decided to mention it to his brother when next he saw him. If his idea should turn out to be right, what was the reason for the feud, and who was behind it? And how did the disappearance of Diana Fielding fit, and that extraordinary business of the telegram? Had she gone because she was in league with the person who was working against Coyne? The fact that she had been the sender of the telegram that had arrived while Paul had been interviewing the man seemed to point to this, but nothing that Bob could think of offered an explanation for the shaven heads.

That was the most extraordinary feature of the whole business. It obviously had a very definite significance, otherwise the sight of the paragraph would never have sent Coyne into a fit. But what could the significance be? Why should any sane man, murderer or otherwise, go to the trouble of shaving the heads of his victims? It was nonsense, unless . . .

Bob's eyes narrowed and his pace perceptibly lessened. Unless it was done to issue a warning to Coyne.

Had he stumbled on the real reason? It was probable. Had the killer performed that inexplicable operation for the sole purpose of letting Coyne know who was responsible? It seemed a very reasonable explanation, and Bob was rather pleased with himself. So far as he could see, it was the *only* reasonable explanation.

He was still turning the theory over in his mind when he reached the tobacconist's and made his purchase. Almost unconsciously, he dawdled on his return journey. The suggestion that had come to him gave him plenty to think over, and he had no particular desire to return to the house before it was absolutely essential.

He strode thoughtfully along, one of the cigarettes he had just bought between his lips. This possible way of accounting for the puzzle of the shaven heads became more possible the longer he thought about it. Linked with the other idea of the feud against members of one family, it supplied an almost perfect theory.

By the time he came within sight of the house, Bob was convinced that he had struck the right solution. It accounted for everything, even Coyne's obvious agitation at being recognised by Alf Weepers. Naturally, if he had changed his name to Coyne with the idea of concealing his whereabouts from the person he feared, recognition by the crook would come as something of a bombshell. Without a doubt, it was worth suggesting to Paul.

He came round the corner of the high wall that surrounded The Wilderness and in sight of the gates, and as he did so he saw something move in the shadow. His peering eyes made out the figure of a man in a heavy overcoat and a soft hat who had been standing near the entrance, and who had moved a few yards away at his approach. Bob frowned, wondering who this lurking individual might be. It occurred to him that possibly it was a boyfriend of the maid's waiting to escort her back home or take her to a place of amusement.

He'll have a long wait, thought Bob. *She doesn't leave till nine and it's barely eight.*

He came to a halt outside the forbidding entrance gates, and was in the act of raising his hand to the bell when the waiting man, evidently making up his mind, came towards him quickly.

'Excuse me,' he said to Bob's surprise, 'but I saw you come out of there a little while ago, and I waited for you to come back. You're staying with Mr. Coyne, aren't you?'

Bob could dimly make out the speaker, a youthful good-looking man of between twenty-eight and thirty. 'Yes,' he replied.

'Could you tell me,' went on the other anxiously, 'whether — whether Miss Fielding's all right? She isn't — ill or anything, is she?'

Bob dropped his hand from the button of the bell without pressing it. 'So far as I know she's quite well,' he answered slowly. 'She's not living here now, you know.'

His questioner uttered an exclamation. 'Not living here?' he echoed. 'What do you mean?'

'If you'll tell me what authority you have to ask,' said Bob, 'I might augment that statement.'

The other eyed him narrowly, and there was a moment's silence. 'Look here,' he said at last, 'I want to hear more about this. What position do you occupy in that household?'

'That,' said Bob coolly, 'is my business. I don't see — '

'I'm not asking just out of curiosity,' broke in the stranger impatiently. 'But what you tell me has worried me. I'm anxious about Diana.'

'Why should you be anxious about

her?' asked Bob, and again the other hesitated.

'Well, I'll risk explaining,' he said. 'I don't know how thick you are with Coyne, but you look a decent sort of fellow. My name's Royden — Jim Royden — and I live over in one of those houses.' He jerked his head vaguely towards the dark expanse of the common. 'I got to know Diana a year ago. I used to watch her when she went down to the village shopping, and eventually we got to nodding to each other and then to speaking. It always struck me that she was pretty unhappy, and one day she admitted it. Her guardian, this fellow Coyne, didn't treat her too well. Whenever she could get out, which wasn't very often, and then only to go to the village and buy something, we used to meet, and — and — well, we got friendly. She never really complained, I don't want you to think that; but from one or two hints she dropped I could tell she didn't have a very good time. How could she, anyway, being shut up in a prison like this place? We got friendly, I told you, and — well, she promised to marry me.' He jerked out this last admission quickly as though it rather embarrassed him to speak about it. 'And now,' he went on, 'you tell me she's gone. What do you mean by that?'

'Just what I said, Mr. Royden,' answered Bob. 'Miss Fielding disappeared some time during last night.'

'Do you mean that?' Royden gripped him by the arm. 'How do you mean, she disappeared?'

Bob thought rapidly and made up his mind. Quickly, and without waste of words, he told the anxious man before him exactly what had happened, and his story did nothing to relieve Jim Royden's anxiety.

'I don't believe it!' he declared when Bob had finished. 'I don't mean that I don't believe you; I mean that I don't believe she went of her own free will. If she'd have been contemplating such a thing, she'd have told me. I don't like it at all. If Diana Fielding left this house, she left it because she was taken away by force!'

14

The Mystery of Diana

Bob was a little startled at Royden's vehemence. It struck him as a peculiar coincidence that his brother should also have hinted at the same thing. 'I don't see how it's possible, Mr. Royden,' he said seriously. 'Force would have necessitated a certain amount of noise, and I heard nothing.' He hadn't thought it necessary to inform the other of the alarm in the night that had resulted in the discovery of Mr. Weepers.

'All the same,' said Royden doggedly, 'I'm certain there's something wrong.'

Bob was undecided. There was certainly a great deal in favour of Royden's argument, but against it was the fact that he had been an inmate of the house, and that he had heard nothing to warrant the suggestion that Diana's disappearance was not voluntary.

'I'll admit it's curious,' he said, 'but at the same time I'm sure there must be another explanation. I myself was able to trace Miss Fielding's footsteps as far as the wall, and hers were the only footsteps inside the garden. There were signs, as I told you, of a car having waited, and it's fairly certain there must have been somebody to help her over the wall. If any force was used, it must have been after she'd climbed the wall.'

'Maybe you're right,' muttered Royden, but he sounded unconvinced. 'Anyway, I'm certain there's something wrong, and I think something ought to be done about it.'

'Look here,' said Bob, 'I'll have to go now. I've already kept dinner waiting. Suppose I meet you some time tomorrow morning and have a further talk about this?'

Royden accepted the suggestion with alacrity. 'Right!' he said. 'What time and where?'

Bob considered. 'I'll walk down towards the village at ten,' he said after a short pause. 'You be on the lookout for me, and we'll go in somewhere and have a cup of coffee.'

The other agreed, gripped Bob's hand, and hurried away into the darkness of the night.

Bob waited for a moment and then pressed the bell. There was some delay before Gunter appeared to open the gates, and during this time he thought over the latest development. This meeting with Royden had certainly deepened the mystery of Diana's disappearance. If the man was speaking the truth, and he had no reason to doubt it, it was certainly unlikely that she would have gone away without notifying him. But if she hadn't gone of her own free will, who had been responsible for her disappearance? Who was the man in the waiting car that had stood opposite the place where she had climbed the wall?

The rasp of the lock broke in on his musings, and Gunter swung back the heavy gates. 'Been wondering where you'd got to,' he said. 'Dinner's been ready these last fifteen minutes.'

Bob murmured an apology.

'Oh, I don't mind,' said the servant, 'but the guv'nor was getting a little irritable.'

Bob soon discovered as he entered the dining-room that Mr. Coyne's irritability was due more to uneasiness than anything else.

'I was afraid something had happened to you,' he said when the young man took his place at the table. 'It took you a mighty long time walk to the village and back.'

'What did you think was likely to happen to me?' asked Bob.

Coyne made a gesture. 'I don't know,' he answered evasively, 'but it's a dark and lonely stretch and — well, you know why you're down here, and it's quite possible that other people know, too.'

'You mean this unknown person who's made three attempts on your life?'

Coyne nodded reluctantly. 'Yes, that's what I was thinking.'

'I should think it very doubtful whether he would have any animosity towards me. I wish there was something more concrete to go on. I suppose you haven't succeeded in remembering anything that would give a clue to the identity of this person?'

Coyne shook his head. 'No. I haven't the remotest idea who it can be.'

The maid arrived with the soup, and he relapsed into silence. Bob, who saw that no good could be gained, did not press the matter further.

The meal was even worse than the one on the previous night. The soup was too salty, and the cutlets that followed were almost burnt to a cinder. The only thing that was at all palatable was the cheese. Coyne, however, seemed to be completely unaware of the unappetising appearance of the food, mechanically eating everything that was set before him without comment. He was a little more communicative than he had been the night before. At one period of his life, he had apparently been in Cape Town, and possessed a considerable knowledge of diamond mining. Whether he had been personally connected with the industry he didn't say, but he seemed to know all about it, and talked interestingly on the subject.

The maid had just brought in the coffee when Gunter appeared with a letter, which he handed to his master. 'Just come by the last post,' he announced in his surly, unpleasant voice, and Samuel Coyne took the envelope. Watching him, Bob saw him frown at the superscription for a moment before he inserted his thumb beneath the flap and ripped it open.

'Excuse me,' he muttered as he withdrew the single sheet of paper it contained, and rapidly ran his eyes down the lines of writing. His frown deepened and his lips compressed. Into his sallow cheeks came a little spot of colour, and Bob guessed that something the letter had contained had made him angry. He said something below his breath that was suspiciously like an oath, and crumpling the letter, thrust it into the pocket of his jacket. 'Would you mind pressing the bell?' he said; and when Bob had obeyed and Gunter appeared in answer to the summons: 'Take me to my study.'

The man wheeled him quickly from the

room, and Bob heard the study door close. Passing it a few seconds later, on his way upstairs to his room, Bob heard the rumble of Coyne's voice, and guessed that he was telephoning. He would have given a lot to have known the contents of that letter which had so annoyed his host. Quite possibly it might not have anything to do with the mystery concerning the man, but on the other hand it might. Obviously it contained something urgent that had to be answered at once.

Bob picked up the book that had been his object in coming to his room, and returned downstairs. There was no sound from behind the closed door of the study now, and making his way to the shabby drawing-room, he settled himself in a chair in front of the meagre fire and attempted to pass the remaining hours before bedtime as best he could.

Samuel Coyne had apparently decided not to put in another appearance that night, for Gunter, when he came in with some coal later, offered the information that Mr. Coyne begged to be excused as he had some work to do. Bob was rather pleased than otherwise, for he preferred his own company to that of the man at whose behest he had taken up a temporary abode in this gloomy and unpleasant house.

He read for some time, trying desperately to concentrate on the printed page, but his thoughts kept straying away to the business on which he was engaged. He found himself once more thinking of Diana Fielding, and trying to fit her disappearance into the theory that had occurred to him on his way to the village. And he found it difficult. Unless she had gone of her own free will, he could discover no reasonable explanation for her absence. In spite of Royden's conviction that she had been forcibly abducted, Bob could not set aside the evidence of his own eyes.

There was no doubt at all that Diana Fielding had walked from the house to the wall surrounding the garden alone and of her own volition. The footprints had been clear, and there was no sign of hesitation about them. Neither had there been the slightest trace of any other footprints near them. Whatever may have happened to her after she had left the confines of the garden, until that moment, she had been a free agent. And the fact that her suitcase was missing showed clearly that she had intended to leave, otherwise she would not have packed before making her exit from the sleeping house. And yet there was something queer about her sudden departure. Even Paul had commented on it.

Bob went up to bed that night in a restless mood. His lack of sleep had made him physically tired, but his brain was active. He wondered if the night would pass without disturbance. The fourth attempt, which Samuel Coyne declared he expected, hadn't yet been made, and there was no indication of when it would.

He looked out into the darkness before undressing, and discovered that a drizzle of rain had begun to fall. And as he looked, he heard the front door open, and presently saw Gunter appear with a lantern. The man moved slowly, pausing every now and again, apparently doing something to the ground.

Bob was puzzled at first, and then he guessed what the servant was doing. He was setting the trip-wires and alarms for the night. He watched the faint light of the lantern dancing about in the darkness of the garden until Gunter returned into the fan-shaped ray of light that came from the open front door. It was blotted out as the door was closed; and pulling the curtains over the window, Bob undressed and got into bed.

His last conscious thought was of the alarm above his head. Would it ring tonight as it had done before, or would the hours of darkness pass without interruption?

With the question in his mind he fell asleep, and he slept dreamlessly, for nothing happened that night to disturb his rest. The tragedy that was to be enacted within sight of that cheerless house was as yet only in its embryo state, and the shadow of death that was creeping nearer was not to touch The Wilderness until another thirty-six hours had passed.

15

Paul Rivington Has an Idea

After the unsuccessful interview with Mr. Weepers at Scotland Yard, Paul Rivington returned to Hampstead a disappointed and thoughtful man. He was tired after his strenuous day, and glad to settle himself in an easy chair before the cosy fire in his study.

He had hoped the burglar would have been able to supply some important information concerning Coyne. That he was in possession of such information, he had no doubt; nor was he under any illusion regarding the reason he had kept silent. Although Mr. Weepers's mentality was below the average, he was sufficiently intelligent to realise that so long as he kept his information to himself, Coyne or Kilroe was a profitable source of income, and once he revealed what he knew, this income would be lost to him. His attitude

196

in the circumstances, therefore, was quite understandable. The question was, what did he know?

Paul lit a cigarette, and leaning back in his chair, mentally went over all the facts in his possession. But he failed to reach any fresh theory that would fit them. The key to the puzzle was missing, and until it was found, the whole business would remain obscure. The nucleus of the mystery — or so he believed — was to be found in the reason for Coyne's fear. That was the centre from which everything else radiated. Once that was made clear, he was convinced the rest would be clear, too.

The identity of the second dead man might help, but there was no knowing how long this might take to discover. It was just as he was preparing to go to bed that the idea occurred to him by which this might be facilitated. It was by no means a certainty, but it was worth trying. He went to bed determined to put the idea that had suggested itself into execution first thing in the morning.

He was up early, and as soon as he had

had breakfast and dealt with his mail, he put through a call to Scotland Yard. Round Robin had just arrived, and he was switched through to the inspector's office.

'I thought of something last night,' he said after they had exchanged preliminary greetings, 'that might help you in discovering the identity of the man who was found at Wimbledon. I suppose you haven't got any further with that yet?'

'No,' answered Mr. Robin disgustedly. 'What's this idea of yours?'

'Well, it struck me that since there are already two Kilroes in this business, there might quite probably be a third.'

'You mean,' said the inspector quickly, 'that the name of the man we found on Wimbledon Common might be Kilroe, too?'

'Yes.'

'What's at the back of your mind?'

'Nothing!' declared his friend candidly. 'It's just an idea of mine and nothing more. If it should turn out to be correct, I have no theory to account for it, but it's worth trying.'

'I'll get on to it at once,' said Mr. Robin, and rang off.

Paul had one or two matters to attend to that morning, which occupied him until lunch-time, and he dismissed the matter of the frightened Mr. Coyne and the men with the shaven heads from his mind.

He had just finished lunch when the telephone bell rang, and Round Robin's piping voice came over the wire. 'If that was only a hunch of yours, it was a pretty good one,' said the inspector. 'You were right, Mr. Rivington, though whether it helps us or not I don't know. Acting on your suggestion, I looked up the London postal directory. There are two Kilroes — one, the fellow who was found by the side of Spaniards Road, James Kilroe; and the other, this poor chap we took to Wimbledon Mortuary.'

Paul's eyes gleamed as he listened. 'You've been pretty quick,' he said.

'We don't let the grass grow under our feet once we've got a line to work on,' said the inspector complacently. 'As soon as I found out there were two Kilroes, I went along to the address of the other. His Christian name was Charles, and he lived in a small house in Camden Town. He was a bachelor and his house is run by a housekeeper. We got hold of her, discovered he hadn't been home all night, and took her along to see the body. She identified him immediately.'

'That's very interesting,' murmured Paul thoughtfully.

'Maybe. But how much further does it get us? It merely makes the thing more difficult.'

'Possibly, at first sight.'

'At first sight or second sight. So far as I can make out, there's no connection between these two fellows except that they bear a similar name. Anyway, Charles Kilroe's housekeeper had never heard of James Kilroe, and James Kilroe's wife had apparently never heard of Charles Kilroe. She's certain he wasn't a relation of her husband's, and the housekeeper swears that to her knowledge, her master had no living relatives. It doesn't make sense, Mr. Rivington. Why should somebody go around killing people just because they're called Kilroe?'

'You don't expect me to answer that, do you?' asked Paul. 'Because if you do, I can't. There may be some connection between the two men that hasn't come to light yet.'

'I'm instituting enquiries about that. The housekeeper supplied us with the address of a firm of solicitors who apparently dealt with the dead man's business. I've got an appointment with them in half an hour, and I'm going to see if anything can be learned there.'

'If you discover anything, you might ring me up again.'

'I will,' promised the inspector.

Paul was frowning as he put the receiver back on its rest. His idea had been more or less a shot in the dark, and yet it had hit the mark. What construction could be put upon this new discovery? Here were two men who, so far as had been discovered, were not related, who had been killed under exactly similar circumstances. The body of one had been found by the side of Spaniards Road, the body of the other on a secluded portion of Wimbledon Common. They had both died from stabbing, and within a few hours of each other, and both their heads had been shaved. The only apparent connection between them was that they each bore the name of Kilroe.

What linked them together and supplied a motive for their deaths? And what linked them to the frightened Mr. Coyne at Datchet, whose real name was also apparently Kilroe, or who at any rate had been known to Weepers as Kilroe?

He spent the entire afternoon trying to evolve a theory, but failed to find a satisfactory one. Just before tea, Round Robin rang up again with the information that he had seen Charles Kilroe's solicitors, but they could offer no suggestion as to the motive for his death. He had been a quiet unassuming man with a small private income, and possessed no living relatives of any description. They were convinced that he had had no business with James Kilroe, although they could not of course definitely state that he hadn't known the man. The interview, from the point of acquiring information, had been wholly unsatisfactory.

'And there we are,' the inspector concluded despondently. 'We know who the dead men were, but it doesn't get us any further. I'm instituting enquiries into their past lives. Perhaps that'll lead to something.'

His tone suggested that he hadn't very much hope that it would lead to anything, and his friend could not offer any solace for this outlook. 'Cheer up, Robin,' he said to the gloomy inspector. 'Usually when a thing looks most hopeless, something happens to straighten it out.'

'I know,' said Round Robin sceptically. 'Always darkest before the dawn business. But if we can straighten out this tangle we'll be clever.'

'Or lucky! You say there are only two Kilroes in the directory?'

'That's all. Why, do you want to find some more?'

'No,' said Paul slowly, 'but I was wondering if our unknown murderer might want to find some more.'

'What are you getting at now? Another idea?'

'No, I should scarcely call it an idea. It hasn't reached that stage yet. Let's call it the embryo of an idea.'

'Well, if you can suggest anything that'll help to clear up this business, I shall be only too pleased,' said Mr. Robin, and on that the conversation ended.

Paul returned to his chair and sat staring at the fire. The nebulous idea that had occurred to him wanted serious thought. There might be something in it. If it could be taken for a fact that the only two Kilroes in London had been selected as victims by the unknown murderer — and this seemed fairly certain — there *was* something in it.

He turned it over in his mind, and the more he thought of it the more he liked it. Its success or failure certainly rested on an unknown quantity — the motive for the two killings that had already taken place. Provided the two men who had been killed had died because they were called Kilroe, there was an even chance his plan would be successful. He began to perfect the details.

But before he was destined to put his idea into execution, a fresh clue was to come to light. The person who provided it was a man who had never heard the name of Kilroe, knew nothing of the two murders, was ignorant of the frightened Mr. Coyne, and stumbled on his discovery purely through misfortune.

16

The Murder House

Mr. Septimus Skinner had seen better days. He was constantly urging this fact upon the more companionable of his fellows in misfortune.

'I used to work in a bank,' confided Mr. Skinner, 'until the invasion of the big combines, when I was frozen out.'

Had he been truthful, he would have stated that his fall from the black-coated class had been due to an overindulgence in whisky, and had nothing whatever to do with the combines against which he railed. Certainly no one, looking at Mr. Skinner, would have imagined for one moment that he had ever held a respectable position behind the mahogany counter of a banking establishment.

His greyish hair beneath his battered hat was matted and dirty; three days' growth of stubble covered his weak chin, and his skin was grimy with the accumulated dirt that many weeks without contact with water had ingrained. His clothes were shapeless and weather-stained, his boots a travesty of footwear, and his red-rimmed eyes bleary from exposure to biting winds and the solace with which Mr. Skinner regaled himself when he had touched lucky and was in funds. He eked out a miserable and precarious living by begging and doing such odd jobs as came his way. For many years now he had been on the road, tramping from place to place, sometimes sleeping beneath the inadequate shelter of a hedge, more often accepting the hospitality of a barn or an empty house.

It was a cold, wet night when he came shuffling along a dark but well-kept street on the fringe of Barnet. He was both cold and hungry, although in the ragged pocket of his coat reposed the where-withal to appease his hunger. That day he had earned one-and-sixpence tidying up the garden of a house at Kingston. A portion of this money he had expended on half a loaf and some cheese, and his immediate desire was to find somewhere he could eat his meal in comparative comfort and pass the night protected from rain and cold. So far he had been unlucky. The streets he had passed through consisted mostly of new villas offering no suggestion of shelter for his weary body.

The road he was on now, however, looked more hopeful. It was a road of large and imposing houses, each surrounded with a considerable average of ground, and so far detached from each other as to make each a separate estate. If he could only find an empty one, his problem would be solved.

He quickened his pace, watching short-sightedly for the welcome board that would signify that his search was over. From somewhere in the wet darkness came the faint sound of a clock chiming one; and as the cracked bell vibrated to silence, Mr. Skinner discovered what he was looking for. From the broken drive-gates of a house a few yards ahead of him protruded an estate agent's sign, 'To be Let or Sold'. Mr. Skinner shuffled towards this sanctuary with a breath of relief, paused at the entrance to the drive, and looked up an uninviting shrubbery of overgrown bushes to where he guessed rather than saw the gloomy building.

A quick glance round assured him that the road was empty, and he slipped through the half-open gate. The rain dripped monotonously from the over-hanging branches of the trees as he made his way up the short approach. Experience had taught him to ignore the front of an unoccupied house. It was seldom there was any means of effecting an entrance there. The back always offered more hopeful prospects.

The drive ended in a semicircular sweep in front of the stone portico of the house, but Mr. Skinner turned off into a side path that led round to the rear of the premises. He passed under a rotting pergola, and presently found himself by a kitchen door. It was locked, as he had expected, but a few feet away from it was a window with a broken pane. He put his hand through the aperture, felt for the catch, and unlatched it. A moment later, he had raised the window and scrambled through into the darkness beyond. In one of his pockets he had an end of candle and a box of matches, which he carried for such emergencies; and confident that the light could not be seen from the road outside, he produced these, struck a match, and lit the candle before proceeding any further.

In the dim light he found that he was in a scullery. The stone floor was thick with dust and crisscrossed with innumerable footprints. He concluded that someone had recently been viewing the house, and shuffled over to a door that he anticipated led to the kitchen.

He was right in his surmise. Beyond was a big oblong apartment with a large range and a dresser. Mr. Skinner decided that this would do very nicely for his temporary sleeping quarters. With the door to the scullery closed, nobody would be able to see the light from the back, and it would also be invisible from the front. Holding the candle above his head, he entered and glanced about him.

A moment later, with a white face and the perspiration streaming down his forehead, he was scrambling back through the window by which he had gained admittance, into the wet darkness of the night. He came running blindly down the drive, his breath whistling through his clenched teeth, his only idea to put as great a distance as possible between that horrible house and himself.

Police Constable Pawley, majestically patrolling his beat, heard the crunch of irregular footsteps on the wet gravel and stopped by the broken drive gate, frowning suspiciously. A running figure burst out of the darkness and almost knocked him over. Pawley grabbed the vague form by a thin arm and jerked it to a stop.

'Now then, what's the idea?' he demanded gruffly.

Mr. Skinner gave a breathless gasp and tried to twist himself free. 'Let me go!' he whined between his chattering teeth. 'I ain't done nothin'.'

The constable tightened his grip,

unhitched his lantern from his belt with his free hand, and directed a bright ray of light on his captive. Mr. Skinner's appearance did nothing to allay his rising suspicions. 'What was you a-doin' in there?' he asked sternly.

Mr. Skinner's red-rimmed, terrified eyes, blinked in the light. 'I wasn't doin' nothin',' he muttered. 'Just lookin' fer a place to sleep, that's all.'

Pawley was not satisfied with the explanation. The man he held was shaking violently, and was evidently crazed with fear. He considered the situation. 'You was runnin' away from somethin',' he declared after a pause. 'Now come on, what was it?'

Mr. Skinner became incoherent. Wriggling like an eel, he pleaded to be released.

'Don't you be impatient, m'lad,' advised the constable. 'I'm goin' to have a look into this, and you're comin' with me. Somethin' made you scuttle away from that house, and I'm goin' to see what it was.' He took a step towards the drive, dragging his prisoner with him.

'No!' screamed Mr. Skinner thinly. 'I won't go back there! I won't!'

'You shut up!' broke in the constable. 'And do as you're told.'

Mr. Skinner expostulated and struggled, and then, realising that it was hopeless, suffered himself to be dragged reluctantly towards the gloomy house.

★   ★   ★

The insistent burr of the telephone bell awoke Paul, and raising himself on one elbow, he stretched out his hand to the instrument by his bedside. He possessed the faculty of waking in full possession of his senses, and when he put the receiver to his ear, his brain was as clear as if it was noon instead of shortly after six, as the clock near the telephone told him.

'Who's that?' he asked, and the voice of Mr. Robin came over the wire.

'Sorry to disturb you so early, Mr. Rivington,' apologised the inspector, 'but I thought you'd like to know the latest developments. I believe we've found the house where those two men were killed.'

'Where are you phoning from?' asked Paul quickly.

'Barnet police station,' answered Round Robin. 'I don't think there's any doubt that this is the place where the murders were committed. It's an empty house in a lonely road on the outskirts of Barnet, and there are traces of blood and hair in the kitchen.'

Paul was interested. 'I'll come along,' he said. 'Wait for me, will you?'

He hung up the receiver, and getting out of bed, dressed rapidly. A phone call to the garage brought his car to the door immediately, and taking the wheel from the mechanic who had driven it round, he sent the big machine speeding through the still, almost empty streets. In three quarters of an hour after receiving the call, he pulled up outside the police station at Barnet. The inspector was warming himself in front of the fire in the charge room, and nodded a greeting as he entered.

'That's pretty quick,' he remarked. 'I didn't expect you for another quarter of an hour at least. We'll go straight round to

214

this place, shall we?'

Paul agreed, and with a word to the desk sergeant the stout little inspector accompanied him to the waiting car.

'How did you make the discovery?' asked Paul as Mr. Robin climbed into the seat beside him.

'A tramp was looking for somewhere to sleep,' explained the inspector, 'and entered the house through a back window. He saw the bloodstains and bolted like a scared rabbit, running into the constable on patrol. The man went to investigate the cause of his scare and immediately notified his inspector, who got in touch with the Yard. They rang me up and I came along at once. They're holding the tramp, a fellow named Skinner, although I'm pretty sure he knows nothing about it. I've seen him — a poor miserable fellow, frightened to death by what he found.' He issued directions, and Paul turned the car off the main road into a side street.

'You say there was hair as well as blood?' Paul asked.

Mr. Robin nodded. 'Yes. It was because

the constable reported that that they got in touch with the Yard. There's hair all over the floor and a new safety razor in the sink. You'll see when you get there.'

He directed his friend through a maze of streets, and presently into one that was more rural in appearance. At the broken gates of the empty house where Mr. Skinner had so optimistically sought refuge for the night, the car was brought to a halt and they got out.

'This is the place,' said the inspector, and Paul stared up the unkempt drive to the partly seen bulk of the house, just visible between the branches of the closely growing trees.

'Quite a useful place to choose for the purpose,' he murmured, glancing quickly about him. 'Completely secluded and sufficiently far away from any other habitation to ensure nothing being heard.'

'That's what I thought,' agreed Mr. Robin, and he led the way up the drive.

Halfway along the weed-grown gravel path, Paul stopped. 'Did you come by car this morning?' he asked.

The inspector shook his round head.

'No,' he replied. 'Why?'

'There are traces of a car having been driven up here recently,' answered Paul, and he pointed them out. 'That's probably the murderer. He wouldn't have risked leaving the machine outside the gates. He would have driven it up here and hidden it in the shadow of the house. Without lights, no one would have suspected its presence.'

They went on towards the house, and knocking at the big weather-beaten front door, were admitted by a constable. Mr. Robin led the way across a bare dusty hall, down a short flight of steps, along a passage, and into a big kitchen. 'Here you are,' he said, pausing on the threshold. 'Look!'

Paul viewed the dusty boards. Great splashes of blood were mingled with the dust, and strewn about were patches of hair. 'I don't think there's much doubt,' he said, his lips compressed. 'This is the place where the two Kilroes were murdered. I suppose you made a pretty close examination this morning?'

The inspector nodded. 'Yes, but there

was nothing of importance. The razor is a cheap one, the kind you can buy at any sixpenny store; and although there are plenty of footprints in the dust, they're too blurred to be of any value.'

'The fellow must have possessed a pretty good nerve,' Paul remarked. 'He took a tremendous risk. At any moment a constable on patrol might have taken it into his head to have a look round the house, and then he'd have been discovered.'

'Which, I imagine, would have been unfortunate for the constable,' put in Mr. Robin grimly.

'Yes, I think you're right. I don't suppose there's anything you've overlooked, but we might as well make sure.'

Paul began a rapid but careful scrutiny of the apartment. He found nothing, and passed through into the scullery. The razor, with traces of hair still adhering to it, lay in the sink. Picking it up, he subjected it to a careful examination.

'There are two different kinds of hair here,' he announced. 'I daresay you noticed that.'

Mr. Robin hadn't noticed it, and said so. 'And in colour and texture it coincides with what little remained on the heads of the dead men,' he added, rubbing the back of his hand across his lips. 'This is the murder house, right enough, Mr. Rivington. But whether it's going to help us at all, I'm doubtful.'

Paul made no reply, but by the time he had completed a search of the place, he began to share the inspector's doubt.

'There's nothing here at all,' he declared disappointedly. 'The man hasn't left the vestige of a clue behind.'

'I thought he hadn't,' grunted Round Robin, 'but I was hoping that I might be mistaken and that you'd find something I'd overlooked. That's why I rang you up.'

'There's not even a fingerprint. Judging by those marks on the table there — ' He nodded towards a decrepit piece of furniture that had apparently been left behind by the previous tenant. ' — the killer wore gloves.'

'They all do nowadays,' said the inspector wearily. He stifled a yawn. 'I think we ought to see this fellow Coyne. If

219

his name's Kilroe, and he knows anything about this business, we ought to get him to talk.'

'I don't think you'll get anything out of him officially,' said Paul, shaking his head, 'but I'll go down later on today. He's more or less a client of mine, and I have a legitimate excuse. If I bring up the subject of the murders without hinting, of course, that I imagine that he's in any way connected with them, he may let fall some item of information that will be valuable.'

He carried out his intention that afternoon, and was to be very glad he had done so; for at Datchet he picked up the first clue that was eventually to lead him to the truth.

17

Royden Makes a Suggestion

Bob kept the appointment made with John Royden on the previous night. The morning was cold and bright, following the rain, and the excuse that he was going for a walk was accepted by Samuel Coyne without comment. Not that any excuse was really necessary, but he thought it was just as well to offer some reason for going out.

He strode across the common, enjoying the keen air and the early spring sunshine. Passing the gate of the house he guessed was Royden's, his conjecture was verified by seeing the man he had come to meet emerge and walk swiftly towards him. They exchanged greetings, and in the revealing light of day Bob's favourable opinion of the man was confirmed.

John Royden was not good-looking, as his features were too irregular, but his expression was pleasant, and there was a strength about his mouth and a hint of humour in his eyes that amply made up for any deficiency he lacked in pure facial perfection.

'I saw you crossing the common,' he said, 'from my bedroom window. You can almost see the gate of The Wilderness from there. Where shall we go? There's a little café in the high street which at this hour in the morning should be practically empty. Will that suit you?'

Bob nodded, and they set off side by side.

'I've been worrying over this business of Diana,' said Royden, plunging immediately into the subject that was nearest his heart, 'and the more I think about it the less I like it.'

'Have you any definite reason for suggesting that Miss Fielding was taken away by force?' asked Bob.

'Not beyond the one I've given you. I'm sure she would have told me if she'd had any intention of leaving.'

'There might be some very good reason why she didn't do that,' remarked Bob.

'You've got to remember that I was there the night she disappeared, and apart from the fact that the house is protected by a complicated system of alarms, nobody could have forced an entrance without my hearing something.'

'I'm not suggesting anyone *did* force an entrance,' Royden said quietly. 'I'm suggesting that Diana's disappearance has been engineered by that guardian of hers.'

This possibility hadn't occurred to Bob, and he frowned. 'What reason could he have had?'

'I don't know, but I'm convinced he's at the bottom of it.'

'He couldn't have done it without assistance.'

'Is he as helpless as he makes out? I've seen him walking across the common as hale and hearty as any man. So far as I can see, there's nothing to prevent him having recovered from the attack and pretending to be a great deal more helpless than he really is.'

Bob looked at Royden curiously. 'Are you offering this merely as a suggestion or have you anything to go on?' he enquired.

Royden hesitated, then: 'I've nothing definite to go on,' he admitted, 'except that Diana was always afraid of the man. You're a detective, aren't you?' Seeing his astonishment, Royden smiled. 'You needn't be surprised that I know,' he went on. 'Diana told me that a detective was coming down because of several attempts that had been made on her guardian's life.'

'Oh, she told you that, did she?' murmured Bob. It was, he thought, a little indiscreet of her. Even to such an intimate friend as John Royden, it had hardly been necessary to mention the reason for his presence.

His thoughts must have communicated themselves to the man beside him, for he continued: 'You see, she told me everything. That's why I'm so sure that if she'd made up her mind to leave The Wilderness, no matter what the reason was, she would have mentioned it to me.'

'I still can't understand,' said Bob, 'what object Mr. Coyne could have in spiriting his ward away, even if it had been possible to do so.'

'Neither can I!' declared Royden frankly. 'But I'll bet you he has, or at any rate knows all about it. And is it so impossible? You've no proof that she actually left the house.'

'Except her footprints — ' began Bob, but the other made an impatient gesture.

'What do they signify?' he interrupted. 'Nothing! Surely it'd be easy enough to fake footprints with a pair of her shoes. They would have to account for her absence somehow, and if they could make it appear she'd left the house of her own free will, so much the better.'

This aspect of Diana's disappearance hadn't occurred to Bob before, and he was forced to admit that there might be something in it. If, for reasons of his own, Samuel Coyne had wished to get her out of the way, he would most certainly have adopted just such methods as Royden had suggested. Had he actually hit upon the real explanation? Had Diana never left the house at all? It was true that Gunter and he had searched the house from top to bottom, but that didn't preclude the possibility that she might have been hidden somewhere. As Royden had said, the footprints could have easily been faked, as could the traces of the waiting car and the marks where she had apparently climbed the wall.

Once the suggestion that she had never left the house was accepted, it explained a great deal that had been puzzling about her disappearance. Bob hadn't considered the explanation before for the simple reason that there appeared to be no motive for Coyne to have taken such a line of action, and also because the man had seemed genuinely annoyed at the discovery of his ward's absence. But he was prepared to admit that this might quite easily have been assumed; what he couldn't do was think of a reasonable motive. He explained this difficulty to Royden, and had just finished when they reached the entrance to the little café in the high street. The place was empty, and settling themselves at a table in a secluded corner, they ordered coffee. When it had been brought, they continued the subject of their conversation.

'I can't suggest a motive for this man Coyne doing such a thing,' admitted Royden. 'But you must agree there's something queer about him, queer about the whole business, and I don't see why Diana's disappearance shouldn't be part and parcel of it.'

Bob was forced to agree with him. He was all the more ready to disbelieve the outward evidence that Diana Fielding had left of her own accord because Paul himself had hinted that he was not satisfied. Had the same idea that had occurred to Royden also been at the back of his brother's mind? If Diana hadn't left The Wilderness, where was she? Was she still concealed somewhere in that gloomy house, or had Coyne and Gunter got her away during Bob's absence in London on the following morning?

'You've certainly given me something to think about, Mr. Royden,' he said as he sipped his coffee.

'I'm glad, because I'm desperately worried. If I'd anything to go on but mere supposition, I would've notified the police. But without being able to produce any evidence, I don't suppose they'd have listened to me.'

'I don't think they would, and I'm very glad you didn't.'

'All the same, I think something ought to be done. We can't just accept the fact that Diana's gone and leave it at that.'

'It won't be left at that,' said Bob reassuringly. 'Now that you've put forward this suggestion, I shall work on it. I suppose, during the time you've known Miss Fielding, she's never mentioned anything that might offer a suggestion for Coyne wishing her out of the way?'

Royden shook his head. 'No, nothing. I was trying to think of that last night.'

'How long has he lived at The Wilderness?'

'A little over two years,' Royden answered at length. 'About two years and three months, to be exact. I remember because I was interested and watched him move in. It's only recently, however, that he's had that gate put up and the place turned into a fortress. Less than two months.'

'How long have you known Miss Fielding?'

'Six or seven months. That is, to speak to. Of course, I knew her by sight considerably longer.'

'You've never met Coyne?'

'No, never. When Diana and I became engaged, I wanted her to tell him. So far as I could see, there was no reason why she shouldn't. He couldn't have possibly objected to our marriage on any grounds. I've got a comfortable income, and there's nothing that anyone could allege against me. She wouldn't hear of it. She was terrified that if he knew of our acquaintance, he'd refuse to allow her out at all.'

'Why?' muttered Bob. 'Surely he must be sensible enough to realise that sooner or later she'd contemplate marriage.'

'You'd think so.' Royden shrugged. 'But she was convinced that he wouldn't hear of it. When I attempted to argue with her, she got so upset that out of consideration for her feelings, I dropped the subject.'

'Was Gunter with them when they moved in?'

'Yes; he was the first to appear on the scene. Coyne and Diana didn't arrive until after the furniture had been got in and everything was more or less fixed up.'

Bob put several more questions, but although Royden answered willingly, he could offer nothing in the way of helpful information. They left the café and parted ways opposite Royden's house, Bob promising that he would let his new acquaintance know as soon as anything was discovered concerning Diana's whereabouts.

'And for the love of Heaven, try and get hold of something quickly,' were Royden's last words. 'I shall be in a fever of impatience until I know definitely what's happened to her.'

Bob walked back to The Wilderness in a thoughtful mood. His conversation with Royden had opened up a new aspect which, although it didn't tend to clarify the situation, certainly supplied plenty to think about.

Gunter admitted him after a considerable delay, with a surly apology for his tardiness on the grounds that he had been out in the garden and hadn't heard the bell.

Samuel Coyne was invisible. He had shut himself up in his study and was working, so the servant said, though what the work was that occupied so much of his time Bob couldn't conjecture. He thought quite probably it was merely an excuse, and in this he was right, for Mr. Coyne was doing nothing more laborious than sitting in his wheelchair staring at the fire.

Lunch that day was a little late, and in quality on a par with the rest of the meals at The Wilderness. The maid had barely finished clearing the table when Gunter appeared to announce Paul Rivington. His brother's arrival was a surprise to Bob, and apparently an even bigger one to Samuel Coyne.

'Show him into the study,' he ordered; and then, as he manipulated his wheel-chair towards the door, 'Did you know your brother was coming down?'

'No,' said Bob, holding open the door of the dining-room. 'Perhaps he wants to see me about something urgently.'

Coyne made no reply, but propelled himself rapidly across the hall into his study. Bob followed, and found Paul warming his hands in front of the fire.

'I thought I'd come down and see how things were progressing,' remarked his brother. 'There have been no further attempts on your life, I presume, Mr. Coyne?'

'Not up to now, I'm thankful to say,' Coyne said. 'I hope this visit, Mr. Rivington, doesn't mean that you are — er — removing your brother?'

'No, no,' answered Paul. 'I merely came to see if anything fresh had occurred. You've heard nothing of Miss Fielding, I suppose?'

Coyne's face clouded. 'No,' he replied shortly.

'Extraordinary, going away suddenly like that,' murmured Paul, pursing his lips. 'My brother told me about it when he came up yesterday. Where do you think she could have gone?'

'I haven't the least idea,' said Coyne.

'Aren't you making any attempt to find out?' Paul's tone was slightly astonished.

'Surely something ought to be done to try and discover her whereabouts?'

'Why should it? She left of her own accord. If she wants to come back, the house is open to her.'

'But don't you think,' Paul persisted, 'that any friends or relatives she may have should be communicated with?'

'She has neither friends nor relations.'

'Then who was the man she left with?' asked Paul, raising his eyebrows. 'Who was it who came in the car?'

The man in the chair made a restless movement. 'I don't know,' he replied. 'Nor is it any concern of mine. She had a good home, and if she's fool enough to leave it at the behest of some Tom, Dick or Harry, she must please herself. She's of age, and although I'm her guardian, she's entitled to do as she pleases.'

Was it his imagination, thought Bob, or was there a certain amount of uneasiness discernible behind Coyne's words? He couldn't be sure. Perhaps his conversation with Royden had prejudiced him.

'Of course, it's your business, Mr. Coyne,' said Paul easily. 'But, personally, if I were in your position, I should wish to go further into the matter.'

Coyne evidently thought some explanation was due for his obvious lack of interest in his ward's movements. 'I'm feeling a little sore, Mr. Rivington,' he said. 'I've looked after Diana since she was quite a child, and I'm very annoyed that she should treat me in this offhand manner. If she contemplated going, the least she could have done was to have told me. As she didn't consider that necessary, but merely went off without a word, I feel that I'm justified in washing my hands of all responsibility.' He changed the subject abruptly. 'I suppose you've discovered nothing further concerning this extraordinary business of mine?'

'I'm afraid I haven't, Mr. Coyne. It's hardly likely in the circumstances that I should have done, is it?'

'No, I suppose not.'

'You see,' went on Paul quickly, 'there's really nothing to go on. You admit yourself that you've no idea who the person is who has made these attempts on your life, or the reason why. Should a fourth be attempted while my brother is with you, we might be in a position to learn something. Until, however, your unknown enemy makes a fresh move, we can do very little. At the present moment, too, my hands are rather full. I'm assisting the police to investigate two recent murders which offer rather an extraordinary problem.' He was watching Coyne closely as he spoke, and only by a flicker of an eyelid and a tightening of the mouth did the man betray any emotion at his words.

'I think I've read something about it in the newspapers,' Coyne remarked, his voice quite steady. 'One was at Hampstead and the other at Wimbledon, isn't that right?'

'That's right,' said Paul. 'For some unknown reason, the murderer had shaved the heads of the dead men. It's a most unusual case.'

'I read about it,' said Coyne. 'Extraordinary!' The fingers of his right hand were plucking nervously at the wooden arm of his chair. 'The men are unidentified?'

'They *were* unidentified,' corrected

Paul. 'The newspapers haven't got hold of it yet, but the police have succeeded in discovering their names. It doesn't help very much, I'm afraid. In fact it only makes the thing more perplexing.'

'Why?' muttered Coyne. 'Who were they?'

'They were both called Kilroe.'

The effect of his words was startling. Coyne's hand tightened on the arm of his chair until the knuckles showed milk-white and his face went grey and old.

'Kilroe!' he croaked hoarsely, and Paul saw in his eyes a terror unbelievable.

18

The Fourth Mr. Kilroe

'Aren't you feeling well?' he asked with assumed anxiety.

Samuel Coyne pulled himself together. 'Yes, yes, I'm quite all right,' he growled with an effort. 'I'm sorry, Mr. Rivington, but your mention of these men's names startled me. You see I — I — ' He paused, licked his lips, and went on quickly, 'I knew a man called Kilroe. A great friend of mine.'

'Oh,' said Paul interestedly. 'That may be of considerable help. It's possible there might be a connection — '

'No!' declared Coyne hurriedly. 'I'm sure there couldn't be. The man I knew has been dead for some years. He — he died in Jo'burg.'

'All the same, it's possible these men might be relatives, or one of them,' persisted Paul. 'Kilroe is an uncommon name and — '

'The man I knew was an orphan,' interrupted Coyne. 'He had no relations living. No, the name startled me for a moment, that's all. There can be no connection.'

'It's a pity,' said Paul, and the tone of his voice was disappointed. 'I was hoping for the moment that my visit here might have accidentally supplied me with a clue to this strange affair. At the present moment, both the police and I are at sea. An enquiry, of course, is being made into the past of these men, and we hope it may reveal something that will suggest a motive for their deaths. When you said you knew a man called Kilroe, I was congratulating myself that it might help us.'

'I'm sorry to disappoint you,' muttered Coyne. He was still suffering from the shock of Paul's words. Tiny beads of perspiration stood out on his forehead, and his whole body shivered intermittently as the control he was exerting momentarily relaxed.

The detective had no illusions concerning the truth of his explanation. He had manufactured the story of the dead Kilroe merely to offer an explanation for his obvious agitation when the identity of the dead men had been revealed. There might, however, be something in his statement concerning Jo'burg, and Paul followed it up.

'You say you knew this man in Johannesburg,' he remarked casually. 'You've been to Africa, then?'

'I was in Jo'burg for some time, yes,' answered Coyne reluctantly. 'It's many years ago, though.'

'A beautiful and interesting town,' said Paul. 'I've been there several times.'

'Yes, very beautiful,' agreed Coyne. It was evident that he had no wish to discuss the merits of Johannesburg. 'Why — why do you think that the man who killed these — these men should have gone to the trouble of shaving their heads?'

'That's what's puzzling the police,' declared Paul. 'I can't form any reasonable theory to account for it. It lifts the whole thing out of the rut of the ordinary

239

murder, and brings it more into the realms of sensational fiction.'

'It seems to me like the action of a lunatic.'

'I'm rather reluctant to accept that explanation.'

'What other explanation is there? Surely no sane person would do such an extraordinary thing?'

'It doesn't seem like it. Of course, if the killer is a lunatic, it's going to add considerably to our difficulty, because in that case it wipes out the question of motive. Most murderers are caught because the reason for their crime is impossible to conceal. Sooner or later, it comes to light and gives a clear indication of the perpetrator.'

'And you think something of the sort will happen in this case?'

'I'm hoping it will. If it doesn't, then it seems to me very doubtful that the criminal will ever be discovered.'

Paul talked at length on the subject, watching Samuel Coyne narrowly; and when he eventually took his leave, he was satisfied of one thing — there was no doubt concerning the frightened man's connection with the murders. Though exactly *how* he was connected, Paul was unable to say. In spite of his fear, in spite of the terror which the subject had inspired, Coyne had been as anxious to discuss it as he had been disinclined to talk about Diana Fielding's disappearance.

The crimes had possessed a morbid attraction for him, and he was interested in any detail concerning them. If, as Paul was convinced, his own fear was inspired by the man who had been guilty of the murders, this was not unnatural.

He had come down by train, the car having developed a slight oil leak on the way from Barnet, and Bob walked with him to the station. During the brief journey, he told his brother of his meeting with Royden and the suggestion he had made concerning Diana Fielding. Paul listened gravely.

'It wouldn't surprise me at all,' he commented, 'if he was right. When you first told me about Diana's disappearance, it struck me that there was something wrong, and Coyne's reluctance to do anything in the matter only tends to confirm my original supposition. He's not the type of man who'd take it as calmly as he has unless he knew a great deal more about it than he admits.'

'It's a queer business altogether,' said Bob. 'And the queerest part of it is that both those men should be called Kilroe.'

'The queerest part of it,' corrected Paul, 'is the shaved heads. The other's possibly capable of a simple explanation, but I can't see how to explain that.'

Bob came to the conclusion that this was a good opportunity to put forward the theory that had occurred to him during his walk to the village on the previous night. As clearly as possible, he did so.

'It's quite practicable,' agreed his brother when he had finished. 'But personally I'm inclined to think there's more in it than that. In my opinion, the fact that the murderer went to the trouble of shaving these men's heads forms the basic motive for the crimes. One thing's certain: Coyne knows the murderer and the reason why these two men were killed.'

'Then why in the world doesn't he tell us, and put an end to his own fears?'

'Because,' answered Paul, 'I don't think he dares. I think that in some way or other, it would put him in a very serious position. If I read him right, he's frightened of two things. He's scared of this unknown man, and he's scared of the police. He's between the edge of the precipice and the advancing tiger, and he can't do anything except keep still.'

'Don't you think it's curious that this man should have made three attempts on Coyne's life, and then apparently given it up and turned his attention to the other men?'

'Very curious,' agreed Paul. 'It's also curious that the warning telegram should have been sent by Miss Fielding. In fact,' he added a little irritably, 'it's all so curious that it doesn't make sense. Has our unknown killer stopped his murderous campaign, or is he now planning a fourth attack on Coyne?'

'If he is, and carries it out, he's going to get a shock.'

'Don't be too sure of that. You've brought a revolver with you?'

'Yes, it's in my bag,' Bob answered.

'Keep it on you. You may need it.'

Paul relapsed into thoughtful silence, and did not speak again until they reached the station. And then, as the train came in and he was taking his leave, he said: 'Don't forget — keep that revolver within reach night and day. And don't relax your vigilance. I don't know when the trouble will start or what form it will take, but that there *will* be trouble before long I'm sure of it, and it's just as well to be prepared.'

During the journey back to town, he thought over the result of his visit. And his last words to Bob had been inspired by a genuine uneasiness. The two murders already committed were the product of a carefully evolved plan, the final phase of which was yet to be completed. And unless he was altogether wrong, the completion would involve Samuel Coyne. Although he hadn't even the haziest notion of the why and wherefore of this business, this was evident, hence his warning.

His interview with the tenant of The Wilderness hadn't been entirely without result. The information he had extracted concerning Johannesburg might very easily prove to be of the first importance, for so far as this was concerned, he was certain that Coyne had been speaking the truth. During some period of his life, he had been in Johannesburg, and it was not unreasonable to suppose that the strange business had begun in South Africa, the end of which was yet to come.

He reached Waterloo just before half-past five. Passing out of the station, he chartered a taxi and was driven to Scotland Yard. Mr. Robin, a little gloomy and depressed, was sitting in his cheerless office. He brightened a little when Paul came in.

'Hello!' he greeted. 'Any news?'

Paul pulled forward the only available chair and sat down. 'Let's hear yours first,' he suggested. The inspector shrugged his plump shoulders.

'Mine's easily told. I haven't got any! I've had two men trying to unearth something in the past lives of these fellows which might give us a lead, but they haven't discovered anything up to now which could have the remotest bearing on their deaths. James Kilroe was definitely a fence. Enough evidence was found at his office to convict him several times over. The other Kilroe seems to have been a particularly harmless individual. How did you get on at Datchet?'

'Not very satisfactorily,' answered Paul, and he gave the gist of his conversation with Coyne. 'The only point that may prove helpful,' he concluded, 'is this visit to Johannesburg. Send a cable to police headquarters out there and ask them if they can give you any information concerning a man named Coyne or Kilroe. The result may be enlightening.'

'We can do with a little light,' grumbled Round Robin, as he scribbled a note on the pad at his elbow. 'I'll attend to this right away. Anything else you can suggest?'

'Not at present.'

'Three Kilroes,' growled Mr. Robin, shaking his head. 'Two of 'em dead and one of 'em scared to death. It's fantastic!'

Paul smiled. 'Perhaps the arrival of the fourth Mr. Kilroe will help to make things clearer,' he remarked.

'The fourth Kilroe?' Round Robin stared at him in astonishment. 'What d'you mean? Who's he?'

'Mr. Joseph Kilroe from South Africa,' answered Paul quietly.

The inspector frowned heavily. 'Don't know what you're talking about. Who's this fellow? I've never heard of him.'

'But you will,' said Paul. 'You'll hear of him very soon.'

19

The Scream in the Night

Bob stood at the window of his bedroom and peered out into the darkness. There was no rain, but heavy clouds obscured the sky, and he was able to see very little.

The evening had passed uneventfully. Samuel Coyne had appeared for dinner and retired immediately after the meal to his study, leaving Bob to his own devices. The young man had read and thought, and eventually gone upstairs to his room, thoroughly bored. He would have welcomed almost anything to break the monotony, for life at The Wilderness was dreary in the extreme. The rest of the household hadn't yet retired. Coyne was still in his study, and Gunter, occupied with some diversion of his own, hadn't yet emerged from the back regions to attend to his nightly duties of setting the alarms.

Bob was still fully dressed, for he felt less like going to bed than he had ever done in his life. Far away in the darkness, across the common, he could make out a faint light, and wondered if it came from Royden's cottage. While he was still wondering, the light went out, and nothing but inky darkness greeted his eye.

He turned away from the window rather wearily, and stood looking down at the red glow of the gas fire. There seemed nothing to do but go to bed, and slowly and reluctantly he began to undress.

He had been lying awake for some time when he heard movements in the house below, and concluded that Gunter was preparing to shut up for the night. The sounds continued for five or ten minutes, and then ceased. Silence settled down over the house, and Bob, snuggling his head into his pillow, tried to sleep.

It was some time before he succeeded, but presently he dropped into a doze. He awakened suddenly, conscious of an unusual sound. He sat up in bed staring into the darkness of his room. But now he could hear nothing. The sound which had driven away sleep had penetrated to his brain without being definable, and for a moment he wondered whether it had been the outcome of a dream. And then his straining ears heard something; the faint noise of a closing door. Footsteps padded softly along the passage outside the closed door of his room, and presently he heard the creak of a stair.

Slipping out of bed, he thrust his feet into slippers and hurriedly drew on his dressing gown. From the small table at his bedhead he took the loaded automatic which after Paul's warning he had put in readiness, dropped it into his pocket, and crossed swiftly to the door, cautiously opening it.

The passage was in darkness; there was no light anywhere. With his head thrust through the half-open door, he listened again. There came to his ears the faint rasp of a bolt as it was drawn back, followed by the unmistakable rattle of a chain. Somebody was unfastening the front door.

Bob consulted the illuminated dial of the watch on his wrist. Half-past twelve.

Who could be going out at this hour, and why? There seemed to be only one answer to the first part of his question. If Samuel Coyne's rheumatism was genuine, it couldn't be him. Therefore, since the only other occupant of the house except himself was Gunter, it must be the servant who was setting forth on this nocturnal excursion.

Bob crept forward towards the head of the stairs, guiding himself by letting his fingers rest lightly on the wall of the passage. He reached the staircase, and leaning over the banister, looked down into the blackness of the hall. There was no sign of life, no sound of movement, but a cold wind came up to him and warned him that the door was open.

He began to descend the stairs, and presently arrived in the hall. The cold wind was more pronounced, and making his way over to the front door, he found, as he had expected, that it was ajar. Pulling it further open, he squeezed out and paused at the top of the shallow steps leading to the gravel of the drive. The darkness was intense. He could barely see two yards in front of him, and no sound reached his ears. Yet somebody had left the house a few moments ago and could not be very far away.

Bob hesitated, undecided whether to go further afield or return to the darkness of the hall and wait for the midnight excursionist to come back. By doing this, he would discover who he was, but not why he had gone out at this late hour, and it was this which interested him most. The difficulty was that if he went down the drive, he might miss him altogether, particularly if the person, whoever it was, suspected he was being followed and chose to work his way back to the house by a circuitous route.

He was still debating with himself what he should do when from somewhere out of the darkness ahead came a sound that chilled his blood and made the hairs of his neck stir. It was a thin wailing scream — a scream in which pain, surprise, and terror were blended to form a nerve-shattering cry. It came from the direction of the gates guarding the entrance to the drive. Without further hesitation, Bob sprang down the steps and sped along the gravel path.

He thought he saw a dark figure plunge into the bushes near the gate, but it was so dark that he couldn't be sure, and anyway his mind was so completely occupied with the determination to find out the reason for that dreadful scream that even if he had been sure, he would not have altered his original intention.

It occurred to him as he arrived breathless at the gate that he would be unable to open it without the key, but, to his surprise, he discovered that it was already open. He pulled it wide and stared out into the dark expanse of deserted common land. He could see nothing to account for the cry he had heard nor any sound, yet whatever had been the cause of it could not be far away. The cry had appeared to come from somewhere to the left of the gate, and in this direction Bob made a search.

In his eagerness to investigate the sound that had originally awakened him, he had forgotten his electric torch, a fact he bitterly regretted. Its light would have been invaluable at the present juncture. He had, however, a box of matches in the pocket of his dressing gown, and was forced to make do with this feeble substitute.

He had exhausted nearly all of them before he came upon a dim shape almost hidden by a clump of gorse bushes. It was the sprawling figure of a man. He lay face downwards and was ominously still. Bob struck his last match but one, and shielding it with his palm, bent over the motionless form. The light glinted on a wet patch between the shoulder blades. He touched it with his fingertip and it came away red and sticky. His heart jumped painfully. Blood! The man had been stabbed. He could see the narrow slit in the cloth of the jacket.

The match burnt down to his fingers and he threw it away, striking another, his last. With difficulty, he turned the limp sprawling figure on to its back and uttered an exclamation as the feeble light of the match fell on the white agonised face. It was Alf Weepers, and he was dead!

His last match flickered out. Bob stood

in the darkness beside the dead body of the burglar. So this was the reason for that horrible wailing scream. It had been the death cry that Weepers had uttered as the knife had entered his back.

There was no doubt that he was dead. The distorted face and the staring eyes told their own story. Bob had seen too many dead men to be misled. And not only was he dead, but he had been murdered — stabbed between the shoulder blades at that instant when he had screamed his terror to the dark and silent night.

The man who had killed him had come from The Wilderness; that was almost certain. It had been the murderer leaving the house that had wakened Bob in the first place. It had been the murderer returning after his crime whom he had seen plunge into the bushes near the gate, which meant that Weepers had been killed by either Gunter or Coyne; there was no other alternative.

Bob flung away the dead end of the match he was twisting between his fingers and turned back towards the gate. The police must be notified at once. That was the first thing to do.

He turned into the drive and came face to face with a dim form.

'Here! Who are you?' demanded a surly voice, and he recognised it as Gunter's.

'There's been a murder within a few yards of the gate!' snapped Bob. 'I'm going to telephone the police!'

'A murder?' There was a scared note in Gunter's voice. 'Here, wait a minute,' he went on rapidly, grabbing Bob by the arm. 'Who's dead?'

'Weepers,' answered Bob, wrenching himself free. 'That man we found in the garden the other night.'

Gunter expelled his pent-up breath noisily. 'Was it 'im that screamed?'

'Yes,' said Bob; and before the man could put any more questions, he hurried away up the drive. There was a light in the hall, and as he entered, he heard Samuel Coyne's voice calling from somewhere above. It was thin and high-pitched with fear.

'Who's that? Is that you, Gunter?'

'No, it's me,' replied Bob. 'Something

unpleasant has happened.'

'What? I heard a scream. Has some-body been hurt?'

'Somebody's been killed!' said Bob curtly. 'I'm going to telephone for the police.'

The invisible man above uttered a startled exclamation. 'Wait! Wait!' he called urgently. 'Where's Gunter? Send him to me! Why doesn't he come and help me down?'

'Gunter's outside,' said Bob, 'and there's really nothing you can do, Mr. Coyne. This is a police job, and they must be notified at once.'

Disregarding Coyne's protests, he went across to the study, found to his relief that the door was unlocked, and entering, picked up the telephone. In a few seconds he was connected with the police station at Datchet and talking with the desk sergeant. His news created something of a sensation, and when he had been assured that an inspector was on his way, he hung up the receiver and went upstairs to interview Coyne, who was still shouting. The man, his face deathly white, was sitting in his wheelchair, and the first thing that Bob noticed was that he was fully dressed.

'Who — who was killed?' he asked, his terrified eyes searching the young man's face.

'Weepers!' answered Bob shortly. 'He was stabbed to death within sight of the gates.'

'Weepers,' muttered Mr. Coyne, and his shaking hand went up to pluck nervously at his lips. 'Good heavens! Who could have killed him?'

Bob made no reply. He remembered the stealthy footsteps that had passed his door and the figure he had thought he had seen plunge into the shrubbery at the end of the drive. There was little doubt in his own mind that the murderer of Alf Weepers was either the man before him or Gunter.

20

The Telegram

The police doctor rose stiffly to his feet and stepped back out of the circle of light cast by the electric lamp of a constable. 'He must have died almost instantly,' he remarked. 'The knife went in between the shoulder blades, missed the spine, and pierced the heart. You say you heard him scream?'

Bob, who was standing near the local inspector, nodded. 'Yes,' he answered.

'He must have screamed when he saw his attacker,' said the doctor. 'He couldn't have screamed after. I should say he was dead before his body reached the ground.'

The local inspector turned to the sergeant who had accompanied him. 'Search the body, Sanders,' he ordered, and as the man obeyed he turned to Bob. 'You say this fellow's a known criminal named Alf Weepers, sir?'

'Yes,' answered Bob. He had already made his identity known to the police official, and acquainted him with a description of how he had come to discover the body. He had, however, omitted to mention that he had been aroused from sleep by hearing someone leave The Wilderness. He had allowed the inspector to conclude that it was the scream which had awakened him and brought him out to investigate.

'Hm! Queer thing,' commented the man. 'I wonder what he was doing here at this time of the night.'

The sergeant, who had been going through the pockets of the dead man, looked up. 'I think you'll find the answer there, sir,' he said, and handed his superior an oblong slip of paper. The local man took it, and bending forward, held it in the light of the constable's lantern. It was a telegram.

Looking over his shoulder, Bob read the words scrawled on it: 'Be outside the gate at one o'clock.' There was no signature, but the office of origin was Datchet.

The inspector, a thin-faced wiry looking man, puckered up his forehead. 'Funny,' he muttered. 'This is evidently an appointment. It was handed in this morning at eleven-fifteen. I'll make some enquiries at the Datchet office as soon as it's open. This ought to provide a good clue. If we can find out who sent this wire, we ought to be on the way to discovering the murderer of this poor chap. 'Outside the gate' looks as if it refers to that one.' He jerked his head towards the massive entrance of The Wilderness. 'There ain't another house within a couple of hundred yards. What else have you found, Sanders?' He folded the telegram and stowed it away carefully in his tunic pocket.

'Nothing of any importance, sir,' answered the sergeant. 'There's five or six pounds in notes and silver, a cheap watch and a handkerchief. That's about all.'

'Five or six pounds, eh?' grunted the inspector. 'That's a good bit of money to find on a fellow like this.'

'That's what I thought, sir,' said the sergeant.

The inspector grunted again. 'What do you know about the people occupying this house?' he asked, looking at Bob. 'You're staying there, ain't you?'

Bob nodded, and tried rapidly to make up his mind as to how much he should divulge. He had no wish to say too much; at the same time he didn't want to hamper the actions of the police. He had as yet made no mention of the unfortunate Mr. Weepers's previous visit to The Wilderness, or the circumstances in which it had taken place.

'If you're under the impression that they can have had anything to do with it,' he remarked, 'I think you're mistaken. Mr. Coyne is practically helpless from rheumatism, and his servant, who with the exception of myself is the only other occupant of the place, is hardly likely to have had any motive for killing a man like Weepers.'

The local inspector, however, apparently had ideas of his own on the subject. 'Maybe you're right, sir,' he said doubtfully. 'It seems queer to me, all the same.

This telegram makes a definite appointment and mentions the gate. There's not another gate for over a couple of hundred yards, and it was outside this one the man was killed.'

'That doesn't necessarily show that this was the gate mentioned as the meeting place,' argued Bob. 'I presume there are other gates within walking distance? The murderer might quite easily have kept the appointment and walked a short distance with his victim before killing him.'

He was in something of a quandary. It had been absolutely essential that the police should be notified of the crime; if it had been possible to avoid this he would have done so, but it wasn't. At the same time he had no wish to do anything that might react unfavourably against any line of action his brother had in mind concerning the Hampstead and Wimbledon murders. The arrest of Coyne or Gunter for the killing of Weepers might seriously inconvenience both Paul and Scotland Yard. Therefore, although he was convinced in his own mind that one or other of them was guilty, he had no wish

263

that the police should share his suspicions.

'Hm! Well, we'll probably know more about it in the morning,' said the inspector, 'when I've had a word with the post office people. In the meanwhile, I'd just like to put a few questions to Mr. Coyne and his servant. See that this fellow is put in the ambulance, Sergeant. There's nothing more we can do with him.'

'You won't want me?' put in the doctor. 'I'll let you have a report in the morning.'

'All right,' said the inspector. 'I'll come back to the station when I'm through, Sanders.'

He turned away and moved towards the gate of The Wilderness, accompanied by Bob. They found Samuel Coyne sitting in his wheelchair in the hall, nervously sipping a cup of coffee Gunter had apparently hurriedly prepared. Bob had warned the man he must expect to be questioned by the police, and had suggested that unless a direct question was asked nothing should be said about Mr. Weepers's unauthorised entry on the previous occasion; a suggestion Coyne had eagerly agreed to.

'I'm sorry to trouble you, sir,' began the inspector politely but firmly, his keen eyes taking a swift inventory of his surroundings, 'but since this unfortunate affair happened within sight, so to speak, of your front door, I'm afraid I shall have to ask you one or two questions.'

'I don't see how I can help you,' answered Coyne, and there was a perceptible tremor in his voice. 'I was just going to bed when I heard the scream, and that's all I know about the affair.'

'Do you usually go to bed so late, sir?' asked the inspector.

'Well, not usually. I had some work to attend to — one or two important letters that I wanted to get off my mind, and so I sat up and wrote them.'

'I see.' The local man's eyes fixed themselves on the wheelchair. 'You're an invalid, I take it, sir?'

'Partly,' answered Coyne. 'I suffer rather badly at times from rheumatism. When I'm under the influence of one of these attacks, it's impossible for me to move without help. My servant waited up until I'd finished what I wanted to do, and then as usual carried me up to my room.'

'What time would that be?'

'I can't be quite certain as to the time. Somewhere about half-past twelve, I should think.'

'You weren't acquainted with the dead man, I suppose, sir?'

'I don't number burglars among my friends, inspector,' replied Coyne with a short laugh that Bob thought sounded a little forced and unreal.

'No, I suppose not, sir,' said the inspector. 'How did you know he was a burglar?'

'This gentleman told me.' Coyne made a gesture with his hand towards Bob. 'This — er — Weepers is er — was — apparently a well-known criminal.'

'Yes, apparently,' said the inspector. 'I suppose you would hardly have been likely to have known him.'

Bob wondered whether he was going to mention the telegram. Coyne's denial of any acquaintance with Alf Weepers was going to prove awkward if that telegram could be traced as having emanated from The Wilderness. But for the present at any rate, the inspector was evidently intending to keep that discovery up his sleeve, for he said nothing about it.

'There's nothing else you can tell me, sir?' he said, and when Coyne shook his head, 'Then I think I'll have a word with your servant, if you don't mind.'

Gunter was sent for and came, sullen-faced and surly as usual, and like his master fully dressed. His story coincided almost word for word with Coyne's. He had locked up as usual and waited for his employer to finish the work on which he was engaged. He had carried him up to his room, and was about to retire to his own when he remembered that he had omitted to lock the garage door, which was round at the side of the house. He had come downstairs, put out the light, unfastened the front door, and gone round to attend to this duty. He was, in fact, in the midst of turning the key when he had been startled by hearing the scream. He had one eye on Bob while he was making this statement, and the young detective guessed that he had made it more for his benefit than the inspector's. He had offered a complete explanation for his discovery of the open front door, and he silently congratulated somebody for having thought of it. Either Coyne or Gunter must have known that he had come down and found the front door open, and hatched up this plausible explanation between them.

'What did you do when you heard the scream?' asked the local man.

'I was paralysed for the moment,' said Gunter, 'and for a second or two I waited, listening. Then I heard somebody running down the drive. That and the scream fair put the wind up me, but after a bit I pulled myself together and went to see what'd happened. When I reached the gate, somebody turned into the drive, and I found it was him.' He jerked his thumb towards Bob. 'He told me what'd happened, and that's all I knows about it.'

The inspector was apparently satisfied. He put one or two more innocuous questions, and then, thanking them all politely, took his departure.

As the sound of his footsteps receded down the drive, Samuel Coyne heaved a sigh of relief and wiped his damp forehead. 'Thank goodness that's over!' he muttered.

Bob thought his relief was a little premature. He himself was not in the least deceived by the local inspector's apparent acceptance of the stories that had been dished out to him. He was a shrewd man, and Bob was fully aware that he was biding his time until such evidence as the telegram might offer should supply him with an excuse for a further visit.

'You'd better set those alarms,' said Coyne, turning to the waiting servant. 'I don't suppose there'll be any more trouble tonight, but you never know.'

The man hesitated, and Bob thought he was on the point of refusing. But if he was, he thought better of it, and slouched towards the open door.

So the alarms hadn't been set that night. Bob, in his hurry to investigate the reason for the scream, had forgotten their existence, but it had occurred to him later to wonder why he hadn't encountered any. Here was the explanation. They hadn't been set, and for a very good reason. Not only was their presence useful in warning the inmates of The Wilderness of any unauthorised person present in the grounds, but they were equally as effective in giving warning of anyone leaving the house. And that night, someone had wanted to leave undetected. Someone who had gone to keep the appointment made by telegram with the unfortunate Alf Weepers. Who was it — Gunter or Samuel Coyne?

Although the sky was beginning to lighten in the east when Bob finally got to bed, he was up before anyone else in the morning and telephoning Paul. Briefly and clearly, he gave a full account of the tragedy.

'The local inspector here is a pretty sharp man,' he concluded. 'And when he enquires about that telegram and traces it back here, as I'm sure he will, there'll be trouble for Coyne.'

'Don't worry about that,' answered

Paul. 'I'll get in touch with Inspector Robin and see that the inspector at Datchet does nothing premature. So Weepers is dead, eh? I didn't altogether expect that, but it fits in. He knew something about Coyne and was probably putting the black on him.'

'That's what I think,' said Bob, speaking in a low voice; he had no wish to be overheard. 'There's not the slightest doubt in my mind that one of them killed Weepers.'

'If it was Coyne, it means that this attack of rheumatism is camouflage. Be extra watchful for the next day or so. I'm hoping by then we shall be in possession of further information.'

He rang off, and Bob, who was attired only in pyjamas and a dressing gown, made his way back to his room to dress. He would be glad, he thought as he passed along the dark corridor, to leave this gloomy, depressing house.

He was to leave it sooner than he expected, and in circumstances which even his wildest imaginings could not have foreseen.

21

The Cable from Johannesburg

Paul Rivington got into communication with Round Robin immediately after receiving Bob's telephone message. The inspector had already heard about the murder of Alf Weepers and was not in the best of tempers.

'If we had people in the C.I.D. with the intelligence of rabbits,' he spluttered angrily, 'it wouldn't have happened. That fool Ayling lost him when he was tailing him the other night, and we haven't been able to pick him up since.' He had spent a long and weary night at the Yard, which accounted for Paul having been able to get in touch with him so early, and as a consequence was tired and a little touchy. 'All right,' he continued, 'I'll have a word with the inspector at Datchet and see that he doesn't do anything to upset things. Have you got anything fresh to tell me?'

'No,' said Paul, 'not at the moment.'

'What about this fellow Kilroe? The fourth Kilroe you were so deuced mysterious about yesterday?'

'You'll know all about him in good time. I can't tell you any more about him at the moment. You sent that cable to Jo'burg?'

'Yes,' said Mr. Robin. 'There should be an answer today.'

'Let me know as soon as it comes. I think that's going to be important.'

'Good job something's going to be important! This business is getting me down. So far we haven't moved an inch, and I can't see any chance of our doing so at the moment.'

'Don't be pessimistic,' said Paul cheerfully. 'I think we may achieve quite a lot in the next few days.'

'Let's hope you're right. I suppose, as usual, you've got some idea buzzing round your head that nobody else knows anything about?'

'To be perfectly candid, I've got two; but they're both so vague that until I can reduce them into something a little more concrete and practical, they're not worth talking about.'

'I suppose you mean,' muttered the inspector, 'that you're not going to talk until everything's cut and dried and the case is finished. That's the worst of you, Mr. Rivington. You're so confoundedly secretive.'

'I don't believe in presenting a job half finished. You ought to know that by now, Robin. Theories and speculations are all very well, but they're no good to you. Hard, solid fact is the only thing you can take before a jury, and until I've got that, I prefer to say nothing. What's the good of wasting time explaining every idea that occurs to me? A great number of them have to be discarded in the light of later events. It's a sheer waste of energy to discuss a theory until one can feel certain that it's the right one.'

'I suppose there's something in what you say,' admitted Mr. Robin reluctantly. 'Well, let me know directly you have got hold of anything definite. You haven't got to turn in reports to impatient heads of departments who clamour for results.

That's the difference between us. I've got to satisfy my superiors daily that progress is being made, and if I can't, I get hauled over the coals.'

Paul was sympathetic. He had experienced this stringent rule in the organisation of the Yard, and felt for the unfortunate men who had to work as best they could under such difficult circumstances.

He finished his conversation with Mr. Robin, and once he had breakfast, set to work on the plan of campaign he had mentally mapped out on the previous night.

This occupied him until lunchtime, and he had barely finished the meal when Round Robin rang up to say that the expected answer from Johannesburg had arrived.

'It contains some pretty interesting reading,' said the inspector. 'Shall I relay it over the telephone or will you come round?'

'I'll come round,' said Paul, and fifteen minutes later entered Mr. Robin's uncomfortable office.

'Sit down,' said the inspector. 'Take a look at that!' He leaned across his desk and held out several cable forms clipped together.

Paul took them and read with interest.

New Scotland Yard, London, England, Very urgent. Police message — clear the line. Begins:

No knowledge concerning Coyne stop name unknown here STOP James C. Kilroe was employed on the detective staff of Kohinoor Diamond Syndicate STOP was suspected in conjunction with fellow officer Charles Manson of large dealing in illicit diamond buying STOP no definite proof against Kilroe but Manson convicted and sent to Breakwater 1933 STOP Kilroe left Johannesburg end of 1934 for England STOP Manson escaped from Breakwater same year STOP was killed during recapture STOP present whereabouts of Kilroe unknown MESSAGE ENDS

'So that's Samuel Coyne,' said Paul

softly. 'An ex-detective in the employ of the Kohinoor Diamond Syndicate. James C. Kilroe. Notice that, Robin?'

'What about it?' asked the inspector.

'James C.,' murmured Paul. 'Probably James Charles. Can't be a coincidence altogether.'

'Coincidence?' Mr. Robin looked blank for a moment, and then his expression changed. 'I see what you mean. James and Charles were the Christian names of the two men who were killed.'

'Exactly!' The detective nodded.

'I don't see that it indicates anything, though,' grunted the Scotland Yard man, wrinkling his brows. 'If you're under the impression that they were related to the Datchet Kilroe, I can definitely assure you they weren't.'

'I wasn't thinking of that,' said Paul. 'I was thinking of something quite different.'

Mr. Robin had opened his mouth to put the obvious question when there came an interruption. There was a tap at the door, and a messenger entered carrying an envelope, which he deposited on the inspector's desk.

'C.R. sent this along to you, sir,' he announced, 'and they'd be glad if you'd let them have it back as soon as you've finished with it.'

'All right,' said Mr. Robin. When the man had withdrawn, he thrust his fingers into the envelope and withdrew the contents. 'Weepers' dossier,' he said, looking across at Paul. 'It'll be wanted at the inquest.'

'What's known about the man?'

'Nothing to his credit.' The inspector ran his eye rapidly down the typewritten particulars of the dead man's crimes and the comments of those who from time to time had been brought into official contact with him. Halfway through the sheet, he paused and his lips pursed into a whistle.

'What have you found?' asked Paul.

Mr. Robin stabbed with a chubby forefinger at an item in the late Mr. Weepers's brief biography. 'Read that!'

Paul got up, and coming round behind him, leaned over his shoulder. 'Was for some years in South Africa,' he read, and his eyes narrowed. 'For South Africa read Johannesburg, and that's where he met Kilroe.'

'That's obvious. That links him up with the fellow at Datchet all right, and explains how he came to recognise him. But what about the two dead Kilroes? How do they come into it?'

'That's what I'm hoping to be able to tell you within the next few days.'

'That's what I'm most interested in,' said Mr. Robin, rubbing two fingertips up and down his small nose. 'There's not much doubt who killed Weepers. It's the killer of these other two I want.'

'Have a little patience and you'll get him. After all, we're advancing slowly but surely. This is a fresh item of information we've got this morning.'

'I'd prefer a little less slowly and a great deal more surely. While we're on the subject of Coyne, or Kilroe, or whatever he likes to call himself, I suppose there's no danger of him making a bolt for it? I had the dickens of a job preventing Naylor, the local man, from issuing a warrant for the arrest of him and the servant. The telegram making the appointment with Weepers was handed in by Gunter. From the post office woman's description, there can be no doubt. I had the greatest difficulty in stopping Naylor from taking immediate action, for he's convinced that Coyne and Gunter know all about the killing of Weepers, and I must say I agree with him.'

'It seems pretty evident on the face of it,' said Paul, 'but I don't think it would be policy to arrest Coyne yet. As for his making a bolt for it, you need have no fear of that. Bob will see that nothing like that happens.'

When he spoke, he firmly believed what he said, and at the time he had every reason for believing it. The news that was to reach him in the small hours of the morning was so totally unexpected that it was not within the realms of possibility that he could have anticipated it.

22

The Button

Samuel Coyne did not put in an appearance for breakfast, and a weary and in consequence more sullen and surly Gunter than usual informed Bob, in answer to his question, that his wakeful night had exhausted him. He did not intend to get up until lunchtime.

There was in Gunter's appearance a tinge of apprehension, and Bob, knowing what he did, was not surprised. Both he and Coyne must be waiting in dreadful expectancy for some further move on the part of the police. They must be aware that the telegram would be traced sooner or later, and when it was, it would implicate them in the death of the unfortunate burglar.

The maid had evidently heard the news of the murder that had taken place during the night within a short distance of the house, for her eyes were scared, and she went about her duties in a condition of mingled terror and excitement.

The morning was dry and a little cold for the time of the year, and at eleven o'clock Bob decided to stretch his legs and see if a brisk walk would have the effect of removing the woolliness his lack of sleep had produced. Putting on his coat, he went in search of Gunter, and persuaded that disagreeable man, much against his will apparently, to accompany him to the gate and unlock it. When the servant had closed it behind him and the sound of his retreating footsteps had faded in the distance, Bob stood for a moment undecided whether he should walk towards the village or explore the opposite direction.

While he was hesitating, his eyes wandered towards the spot where he had discovered the body of Alf Weepers. And more out of curiosity than anything else, he moved towards this. The rank grass was beaten down and stained where the crook had lain, and trampled by the boots of the official investigators. A trail of brownish-red stains showed where the dead man had staggered a few paces before falling. Whose hand had driven that knife between the thin shoulder blades? It must have required a certain amount of strength; more than Coyne looked as if he were capable of, even if his rheumatism was nothing more than a blind. Such a blow seemed more compatible with the burly Gunter; and yet surely the servant would not have jeopardised his neck for the sake of his employer, or was there something more between them than master and man?

That was probable. It seemed distinctly possible when Bob recollected the way in which Gunter was in the habit of treating his employer. He was by no means the ideal servant. His offhandedness was rude and ungracious. There were times when he was barely civil, and Coyne treated his moods with a consideration and tolerance that he would scarcely have done if there were not some stronger link between them. 'Confederate' seemed a better description than 'servant', Bob mentally concluded. But confederate in what?

The fear that possessed Coyne had no reflection in Gunter; and that Coyne was desperately afraid of something or someone was evident in his every expression, every movement. It was equally evident in the precautions that the man had taken to protect himself from an unauthorised visitor — the heavy gates; the alarms and trip-wires that riddled the grounds at night. Unconsciously, Bob, as he stood staring at the mute evidence of violent death, drew his brows together in a frown. It was intensely puzzling — not the killing of Weepers but what lay behind it. The motive for the murder of the burglar was plain enough. He had known something about Kilroe or Coyne, the knowledge of which was dangerous to the man's safety. He had probably thought that what he knew would bring him easy money, and he had died for his temerity.

The problem was, what had he known? And what relation did the knowledge have to those other dead men bearing the same name as the tenant of The Wilderness, who had been discovered with their heads shaved?

Bob twisted his shoulders impatiently. Well, it was no good standing here puzzling his brain. Gazing at the spot where Weepers had met his death wouldn't supply an answer to his questions.

And it was as he moved forward that he made his discovery. It was lying half-hidden by a tuft of grass — a little dark object that caught his eye and caused him to stoop quickly and pick it up.

For a second he failed to realise the significance of his find, for it was a very ordinary button of dark-coloured bone, quite plain and without ornamentation of any kind. And then he saw the streak of brownish-red that had dried on the smooth surface, and it came to him suddenly that he held in his fingers a possible clue to the man who had passed that way in the darkness of the night and left death behind him.

He examined the button with closer attention. Adhering to the threads was a tiny scrap of blue cloth, suggesting that it had been torn forcibly from the material to which it had been attached. From its size, he concluded that this had been an overcoat. Had Weepers, before the knife had entered his body, made a desperate clutch at his assailant and ripped the button off in so doing?

Bob took out his handkerchief, a clean one, and wrapped the button carefully up in it. It might have nothing to do with the murder, but it was more than likely that it had, and would prove an important clue.

He tried to recollect whether he had seen an overcoat belonging either to Gunter or Coyne from which this could have become detached, but he realised that during his sojourn at The Wilderness neither of them had worn such a thing. With Coyne in an apparently helpless state, it had been unnecessary; and Gunter, to his knowledge, had never gone out. Whoever had sent that telegram from the Datchet office must have taken advantage of his absence when he had gone to meet Royden. The fact, however, that he had never seen such a garment did not preclude the possibility of its existence.

The thought of Royden sent his eyes in the direction of the house he occupied, and caused him to wonder whether he might meet him again. He stowed the handkerchief containing the button carefully away in his breast-pocket and walked slowly towards the village. Possibly Royden might see him — he had mentioned that from his bedroom window he could see the gate of The Wilderness — and come out for a chat. Bob would rather have welcomed his appearance, but he reached the edge of the common without seeing a sign of him.

The clear air had done much to remove his tiredness. His eyes still smarted a little, but his brain was as clear and alert as it had ever been. He walked as far as the railway station, and then set off on his return journey. As he came in sight of The Wilderness, he saw that the gate was open and Gunter was standing on the threshold looking towards him. The servant advanced to meet him as he approached. When he came within speaking distance, his greeting gave Bob something of a shock.

'What was that you picked up,' he said, 'at the place where that feller was killed?'

'Picked up?' Bob repeated the words to give himself time to think.

'Yes!' said Gunter roughly. 'I saw yer. I was watching through the trap in the gate. You picked something up. What was it?'

'I don't see that it's any concern of yours,' said Bob coolly. 'But if you must know, it was a shilling. Probably it dropped out of Weepers's pocket when he fell.'

The burly man looked at him suspiciously, and there was disbelief in his eyes. 'Oh, was that what it was? I thought — ' He stopped himself abruptly.

'What did you think?' demanded Bob.

'I thought maybe you'd found something that 'ud tell who stuck the knife in the chap.'

'If I had,' said Bob shortly, 'I should notify the police.'

He walked on towards the gate with Gunter at his side. The man was openly dissatisfied and curious.

'Is that where you went to — the police?' he asked, after a pause.

'No!' snapped Bob, a little irritable at this cross-examination. 'I went for a walk. I went as far as Datchet station, turned round, and came back again. Now are you satisfied?'

The servant muttered something under his breath. It might have been a mumbled apology, but Bob was sceptical. They passed together into the drive, and Gunter stayed behind to shut and lock the gate. Entering the house, Bob went straight upstairs to his room and made another examination of the button. It would be something, he thought, if he could find the coat to which it belonged. Though if it had been missed, there was little hope of that. Such a damning piece of evidence would have been destroyed at once.

He replaced his find in his pocket, and coming downstairs stopped by the hall-stand. There were two overcoats and a mackintosh hanging on this, but none of them were of the same material as the little shred of cloth attached to the button.

He was still looking at the hall-stand

when Gunter came in and closed the door. Bob thought the man was going to say something further, but he only gave him a sharp look and passed on in the direction of the kitchen.

The young man strolled into the drawing-room. There was still no sign of Coyne. He concluded that he was still in bed. It occurred to him to ring up his brother and acquaint him with his discovery, and he wished afterward that he had put this suggestion into execution. The only reason that prevented him was the uncertainty of being able to talk in complete privacy, and he had no desire for a possible eavesdropping Gunter to overhear his conversation.

Lunchtime came, and with it a message from Coyne delivered by the maid, asking Bob to excuse his absence. The shock of the previous night had upset his nerves, and he thought it would be better if he remained where he was for the rest of the day. Bob sent back a regretful message, but welcomed the opportunity of eating the meal alone. He had plenty to occupy his thoughts, and Coyne was not a very cheerful companion, anyhow.

He had his lunch in solitary state and returned to the drawing-room, settling himself in a chair in front of the fire with the intention of concentrating his mind on the puzzle. But the warmth and comfort of his chair brought back a recurrence of his previous tiredness which his walk had eradicated. He found himself nodding. His thoughts strayed away into oblivion, and he slept.

He awoke to find the maid setting down a tea-tray on a low table beside his chair.

'Will you have the lights on, sir?' she asked. 'Or will you be able to see?'

It was beginning to get dusk outside, but the room was by no means dark. 'No, I think it will be light enough,' said Bob. 'You might put some more coal on the fire.' It had burned down to a red glow, but as she obeyed, it leaped into a cheerful blaze.

The sleep had done him good, and he felt refreshed, a feeling that was enhanced when he had finished his tea. He wondered whether Coyne was coming down for dinner, or whether he proposed to remain where he was throughout the evening as well.

The maid came to take the tea things away and Bob was left alone until nearly six, when he heard the telephone bell ring, and presently Gunter put in an appearance.

'It's for you,' he said, and his face was perturbed. 'They're ringing up from the police station.' Bob was a little surprised. When the morning and afternoon had passed without a return visit from the inspector, he had concluded that Paul, through Mr. Robin, had arranged matters satisfactorily. What could they want him for?

He followed Gunter into Coyne's study, and picked up the receiver which the man had laid down beside the telephone instrument. 'Hello!' he called.

'This is the station sergeant speaking,' said a rough voice. 'inspector Naylor wants to see you. Could you come along to the station at once?'

'What does he want to see me about?'

'I couldn't exactly say, sir. But he told

me to tell you it was urgent. It's about the murder last night.'

'All right. I'll come along now.'

'The inspector can expect you in about half an hour, then, sir?' said the voice, and after confirming this, Bob rang off.

Gunter, who had been hovering in the doorway, addressed him as he turned. 'What did they want?'

'I don't know,' answered Bob. 'They want to see me, that's all. Will you come and unlock the gate for me?' The servant nodded. 'I wonder what they want,' he muttered. But Bob had no notion himself, and he couldn't, even if he had wished, offer a suggestion.

It was quite dark when he followed Gunter down the drive and watched the servant unlock the gate.

'You'll be back in time for dinner, I suppose?' grunted the man.

Bob nodded. 'Yes, I expect so,' he answered, and swung off across the deserted common.

He was puzzled concerning the reason for this urgent request on the part of Inspector Naylor, although a little thought showed him it was quite understandable. No doubt, although Mr. Robin had prevented any premature action on the part of the local police, they were still anxious to acquire all possible information. It occurred to Bob that most probably what they wanted to see him about was Weepers's previous presence at The Wilderness, for they were no doubt fully aware of that by now. Mr. Robin had probably told them all about it when he had put forward his request for no immediate action to be taken.

Bob walked quickly, and was halfway across the common when some instinct warned him that he was being followed. He stopped, swung round, and caught sight of a dim, vague figure in the darkness behind him. Even as he became aware of it, the figure rushed towards him, a silent blot of shadow. He saw the arm upraised to strike, tried to fend off the blow, failed, felt something crash on the back of his skull with a force that sent him staggering, was conscious of a violent pain that seemed to shoot down his spine, and then was conscious of nothing more . . .

23

The Man with the Squeaky Voice.

Bob opened his eyes with a groan. The lids were heavy and sore, and the whole of his head throbbed painfully. There was an unpleasant sick feeling in the pit of his stomach, and surges of nausea swept over him when he tried to move. From somewhere a dim light illumined a sparsely furnished bedroom. He discovered, although the effort to keep his eyes open was agony, that he was lying on a narrow bed with his wrists and ankles tied. The light came from a candle on the mantelpiece. Feeble though it was, it seemed to scorch into his brain, and forced him eventually to shut his eyes to gain relief.

Where was he, and what had happened? He remembered the telephone message and setting forth to keep his appointment at the police station, the silent rushing figure in the darkness, and the crashing blow that had jarred his brain and hurled his senses into oblivion. Who had been responsible for that? Gunter or Coyne? He tried to think it out, but he was still dazed, and the effort was too much for him. With closed eyes he lay back, waiting for the effects of the blow to wear off, and gradually they did. The throbbing and the nausea remained, but he found that presently he was able to think more clearly.

Gunter or Coyne? It might have been either. He had had no time to catch more than a vague glimpse of his assailant. He wondered what the motive could be for this surprising attack, and remembered his discovery of the button, and Gunter's interest in what he had found. Was this the reason? Had the servant reported to Coyne what he had seen? Had they decided upon this means of shutting his mouth? However, he couldn't quite see why they should have waited until the police message called him out. Surely it would have been better, and far easier, and less risky, to have carried out their intention in the house?

He opened his eyes again, and found he could bear the light a little better. He presumed he was in The Wilderness, though the room was unfamiliar. He remembered, during his search for Diana Fielding, entering several small bedrooms on the top floor, and decided that this must be one of them.

The back of his head was very sore and painful, and when he tried to shift to a more comfortable position, he winced. He lay listening for some time, but could hear no sound, and, closing his eyes again, he drifted into a semi-doze.

He was startled out of this by hearing a noise outside the door of the room in which he lay. A key rattled in the lock and a man entered. He was dressed in a dark overcoat; a soft hat was pulled low over his forehead, and a handkerchief tied round his nose and mouth concealed his face. For a moment he stood looking down at Bob, his eyes invisible in the shadow cast by the brim of the hat; and when he spoke it was in a high falsetto voice, obviously adopted for the purpose of disguise.

'Conscious, are you?' he said. 'I thought perhaps I'd hit you harder than I intended.'

The man might be Coyne; it was certainly not Gunter. He was taller and less bulky than the sullen-faced servant. 'You hit quite hard enough,' said Bob huskily. 'What's the idea?'

'The idea is to stop you poking about and generally interfering. If you'd been content to mind your own business, you wouldn't be in this position.'

'How long do you intend to keep me here?' said Bob, speaking with difficulty, for his throat was dry. 'When I don't turn up at the police station, they'll start making enquiries.'

The other gave a little chuckle. 'Will they? Don't you have any illusion on that point. They don't expect you at the police station. That was a little idea of my own.'

Bob frowned. 'You mean the message was a hoax?'

'Yes. The man nodded. 'Rather clever, don't you think?'

Bob was bewildered. How had the

message been sent? It must have been telephoned from outside The Wilderness. Who had been responsible for it? And then the explanation came to him — Coyne! The man was not helpless from rheumatism, and the excuse that he was remaining in bed because he was upset over the death of Weepers had been nothing more than sheer bluff. He had been neither in bed nor inside the house. He and Gunter between them had arranged the trap, and Coyne had carried it out. He had telephoned the fake message to bring Bob out of the house, and had been waiting for him on the desolate stretch of common land.

'I suppose,' he said, 'you think you're very clever, don't you?'

'I think it was rather smart.'

'And I suppose, you're under the impression that I haven't seen through it? That I don't realise who you are? You think you're going to bamboozle me into believing that I was attacked by a stranger?'

The other was evidently a little taken

aback. 'What do you mean? Who do you think I am?'

'I *know* who you are!' retorted Bob. 'You're Coyne! All that business about being too ill to get up was just an excuse.'

The man was silent. 'You think that, do you?' he remarked at length. 'Well, I'm not going either to confirm or deny your suspicions. You can think what you like. You'll be able to make very little use of your knowledge, I can assure you of that. Nor will the discovery of the button help you.'

'Oh, you found that, did you?'

'I found it when I searched you. It may interest you to know that it no longer exists. It's just a heap of ash at the present moment.'

'It won't make any difference ultimately. The police know why Weepers was killed.'

The other drew in his breath quickly.

'Yes,' Bob went on. 'They know he recognised you that night I caught him trying to break into The Wilderness. They know it was to keep his mouth shut that you let him go. They guessed that he tried to blackmail you, and because you didn't want him to spread around that your real name was Kilroe — '

He broke off, staring at the man before him. He had uttered a strangled gasp and staggered back as though from the effects of a physical blow. 'Say that again!' he snarled harshly.

'You didn't think I knew that, eh?' said Bob. 'You thought I hadn't heard what he called you. Well, I did; and whether you've burnt that button or not, it won't make any difference.'

'It'll make a lot of difference,' whispered the man when he had recovered from his shock. 'It'll make a tremendous difference. You don't know what a difference it'll make!' He stared fixedly at his captive for some seconds, and then, without speaking again, he turned abruptly and left the room, shutting and locking the door behind him.

*   *   *

Paul Rivington went to bed unusually early, after arranging to be called at six.

The following day was likely to be a heavy one, for he had planned to put into execution the idea that had occurred to him for unmasking the identity of the Kilroe murderer. He had no idea, as he undressed slowly, that the events of the next few hours were to render all his careful preparations unnecessary, and that the murderer was to be delivered into his hands without recourse to the more subtle method that had suggested itself to him. Afterwards, when everything was made clear, he was astonished how near his shot in the dark had been to the truth, and congratulated himself on the knowledge that if destiny hadn't willed otherwise, his method would most probably have proved successful.

He possessed the faculty, acquired by long practice, of making his mind a blank at will, and ten minutes after his head touched the pillow, he was asleep. The strident summons of the telephone bell woke him suddenly; and as he stretched out his hand to the instrument beside his bed, he glanced at the little clock, noting mechanically that it was ten minutes past three. He put the receiver to his ear, and a voice, vibrant with terror, came over the wire.

'Mr. Rivington! Is that Mr. Rivington?'

'Yes,' said Paul. 'Who's speaking?'

'Coyne. For goodness' sake, come down here at once! He's here! He's outside now!'

'Who is?' snapped Paul.

'Manson!' The voice was almost breathless with fear. 'For God's sake — '

'Where's my brother?' demanded Paul curtly.

'He isn't here,' sobbed Coyne. 'He went out early this evening to go to the police station, and he hasn't got back. I — '

A grating, rasping noise drowned his voice, and then there was silence.

Paul Rivington's face set sternly. He had heard that noise before and knew what it meant. Someone had cut the wire.

24

The Murderer

Paul Rivington's big car sped through the deserted streets, heedless of all the speed regulations that were ever invented.

It was barely twenty minutes since the interrupted telephone call had come through, and the detective drove with his mind in a chaotic whirl. What had Coyne meant by Manson? Manson had been mentioned in the cable from Johannesburg, but according to that he had died two years ago, during the efforts to recapture him after he had escaped from the Breakwater. Could this report be false? Was the man still alive?

It seemed incredible. The Johannesburg officials could scarcely have made a mistake. And yet Coyne had said 'Manson' distinctly. And what had happened to Bob?

Paul's nerves tingled in anticipatory

excitement. What would he find in that gloomy house at Datchet when he reached it? It would take him over an hour to get there, even at the speed he was travelling; an hour and a half, since Coyne had put through that telephone message. A lot could happen in an hour and a half. What would he find?

He tore on through the night, the quivering needle of the speed indicator swinging between seventy and eighty, and never dropping below fifty.

It was well under the hour when he thundered over the level crossing at Datchet station and swung round towards the common. A hundred yards from The Wilderness, he brought the car to a stop, climbed out, and covered the rest of the distance on foot. It was just as well that the sound of his engine should give no warning of his arrival.

He passed swiftly along in the shadow of the high wall and came to the gate, trying it softly. It was locked. The panel in the centre was pushed back, and he peered through, looking up the drive towards where he could dimly make out the black bulk of the house. A faint light was visible, filtering out through a lower window. He frowned, considering how best he could reach the place without giving warning of his presence. He had no idea what he might find. The man whom Coyne had mentioned, if he was there, would have to be taken by surprise. He felt in the pocket of his overcoat, and the cold butt of the automatic he carried was reassuring to his fingers.

He moved along the wall, looking for a likely place to climb over. Presently he found one. With a light spring he caught the parapet, pulling himself up until his chest was resting on the top of the brickwork. From this position, it was easy to wriggle himself forward until he was able to sit astride. A second later, he had dropped softly into the shrubbery on the other side. Remembering the precautions Samuel Coyne had taken to safeguard his house from any form of intrusion, he advanced carefully, watching for the stretched wires that would notify the inmates that someone had entered the grounds. He found several and stepped over them.

He could see the window now from which the light shone forth. It came from between a pair of heavy curtains that hadn't been drawn quite closed, and the suggestion it offered was obvious. Cautiously and silently, he crept towards that lighted window, and presently found himself beneath it. By craning his neck, he could see into the room beyond, and found that he was looking into Samuel Coyne's study. The sight that met his eyes caused him to catch his breath. On the floor lay the figure of Gunter, face downwards, and ominously still. A little trickle of blood stained the carpet beside him, and Paul guessed he was either dead or seriously injured. Sitting in a chair, his arms and feet tightly secured, was Samuel Coyne. His eyes were starting from his head with fright, and his face was the colour of dirty paper. He was staring fixedly at the figure of a man who stood in front of him, his back to the window. The man was speaking, and by straining his ears the detective was able to catch what he said.

'You've only got a short time, Kilroe!' The voice was high-pitched and rasping. 'Tell me what I want to know before you die!'

The terrified man in the chair babbled something inaudible.

'I'm not here to bargain,' answered the stranger. 'I've made two mistakes, but this time I'm going to achieve my object.'

Again Samuel Coyne's lips moved, but Paul did not catch what he said.

'You can plead as much as you like, but it will make no difference,' said the other remorselessly; and the watcher saw that his right hand held an automatic pistol. 'I've found you at last, and you're going to suffer!'

A stream of words poured from Coyne's ashen lips, but only a slur of sound reached the detective.

'I guessed something like that had happened,' said the man with the pistol, 'though I didn't know the reason. Tell me the address.'

This time Paul heard part of Coyne's reply.

'Seventeen Manette — ' The rest of the

sentence failed to reach him, but his imagination supplied 'street' or 'road'.

'You've told me all I want to know. The rest you can supply without speech.'

The tall figure dropped the revolver he had been holding into the pocket of his overcoat, and his hand went up to his breast. Paul saw Coyne's eyes dilate, and as the other took a step forward, he caught a momentary glimpse of something that glittered in the light. The lips of the bound man in the chair parted.

'No, no!' he screamed. 'Keep away — '

And as Paul realised that it was a knife that the man had drawn from beneath his coat, he acted. Pulling his automatic from his pocket, he smashed the window, and at the same moment with his other hand tore aside the obscuring curtains. The noise of the breaking glass alarmed the killer, and he swung round with an oath.

'Drop that knife and put up your hands!' ordered Paul sharply, his pistol covering the man through the jagged hole.

The murderer hesitated.

'Quick!' snapped Rivington. 'There's

eight shots in this thing, and you'll get them all unless you do as you're told!'

Reluctantly the other let the knife slip through his fingers, and it stuck, quivering, in the carpet as he slowly raised his arms. Paul could see nothing of his face, for it was concealed behind the handkerchief he wore tied over nose and chin.

'Keep still, and don't move!' he warned; and without taking his eyes off the man, he inserted his free hand through the hole in the window pane and fumbled for the catch. It snapped back, and with a quick movement he pushed up the sash. Throwing his legs over the sill, he hoisted himself into the room. 'Now!' he said, and at that moment an unexpected disaster overtook him.

In tugging aside the curtains, he had loosened the rod on which they hung from its support, and as he spoke it fell, the curtains enveloping him in their folds. The room was blotted out. Before he could free himself, he felt a strong hand grip his pistol wrist and twist the weapon from his grasp.

'Now,' breathed a voice exultantly, 'it's

my turn to say something, I think!'

Paul shook the clinging fabric from his head and stared into the muzzle of his own automatic.

'It seems to be my lucky night,' said the unknown. 'What a lot of birds I'm collecting for the killing!' His voice changed suddenly. 'Get over there, against the wall,' he said curtly. Paul, with a slight shrug of his shoulders, obeyed; there was nothing else he could do at the moment. He was unarmed and helpless.

'Mr. Rivington!' The name came in a hoarse croak from Coyne, and the man in the overcoat started.

'So that's who you are,' he said softly. 'Paul Rivington, eh? I was wondering who I had to deal with.'

'Well, now you know,' said Paul coolly.

'Yes, now I know,' answered the other, nodding. 'Well, you're just in time to witness the last act in this little comedy — or perhaps 'tragedy' would be the better word.' He paused, evidently thinking quickly. 'I don't want to have to kill you,' he went on. 'Yet I don't see what else I can do. There's a certain little operation I have to perform before I leave here, and since it will require both hands, I don't know what to do with you while I'm attending to it.'

'It does seem a little awkward,' murmured Paul.

'Indeed. I'm afraid you'll have to die.'

Paul's expression remained unchanged, but he knew he was closer to death at that moment than he had been for a long time.

'Manson — ' began the quavering voice of Coyne.

'Shut up!' snarled Manson, without taking his eyes off Paul. 'Shut up, you cringing rat! You — turn round and face the wall!'

The detective did so, wonderingly. Was it Manson's intention to shoot him in the back? He nerved himself for the shock, but it never came. Instead his hat was suddenly twitched from his head, he felt a waft of air fan his neck, and then something hard crashed with agonising force on the back of his skull. With a shrill scream ringing in his ears, his knees gave way, and he slid limply to the floor.

When his senses came back, he discovered that during his brief period of unconsciousness, Manson had bound his wrists and ankles. His head hurt abominably, a tender rawness that became almost unbearable at the slightest movement. The curtains had been replaced roughly over the window and drawn to, and Manson was bending over Coyne, clipping his hair with a pair of scissors. The man's head lolled helplessly, and Paul's first impression was that he was dead. A second glance, however, enabled him to distinguish a slight rise and fall of the chest. He was only unconscious, and had probably fainted from sheer fright.

Curiously, and without giving any sign that he had recovered from the sudden and unexpected blow, he watched as Manson continued his extraordinary task. He was unable to hazard a guess as to the reason that lay behind the apparent necessity for removing Coyne's hair, and in spite of his unpleasant and dangerous position, he was intensely interested.

The man finished with the scissors,

threw them aside, and, producing from the pocket of his overcoat a safety razor, began to shave the head of the unconscious man. Paul looked on, fascinated. Never in the whole of his experience could he remember such a bizarre scene: the limp, lolling figure in the chair, the masked man behind bending over him, and the glitter of the plated razor in the light.

Incredibly quickly, Coyne's head began to assume the appearance of a bladder of lard; and when the last remaining vestige of hair had been shaved away, Manson uttered a cry of triumph. He flung the razor down, and plunging his hand into his breast pocket, took out a notebook and pencil. As he moved round to get a better view, Paul was able to catch a glimpse of the top of Coyne's now completely bald head; and the instant he did so, the reason for the murderer's strange operation was made clear.

Standing out on the white skin was a blue design, a design that had at some period of Coyne's life been tattooed upon his naked skull.

Eagerly, Manson began to copy it on to a page of his notebook. As he finished and put both book and pencil back in his pocket, Coyne moaned uneasily and opened his eyes. For a moment he stared dazedly about him, a grotesque-looking figure, almost unrecognisable with his hairless head. And then, as he caught sight of the man beside him, the terror came back to his face.

'Manson,' he muttered hoarsely. 'Manson.'

'It would have been better, Kilroe,' said Manson, 'if you'd remained unconscious.' And turning, he walked to where the knife still stuck in the floor. Stooping, he pulled it out and tested the point with his thumb. A gasp of fear escaped the bound man in the chair as he realised his intention.

'No! *No!*' he screamed in a thin, hoarse whisper, as though terror had paralysed the muscles of his throat. 'No! Not that, Manson! I'll do anything — '

'You should have thought of that three years ago!' said Manson. Stepping to his side, he raised the knife.

A shot split the tense silence. With a cry of pain, Manson dropped the knife and clasped his wrist from which the blood was spurting.

'I seem to have arrived at the right moment,' said a voice from the broken window. 'Don't try any tricks, or the next bullet will go through your stomach!'

Manson stiffened; and Paul, twisting his head with difficulty, saw the haggard face of Bob peering in through the broken pane.

25

Behind the Handkerchief

There was a moment of complete silence as Bob finished speaking. Manson stood motionless, his hand still clasping his wounded wrist as though turned to stone at the unexpectedness of the interruption.

Coyne, his lower jaw sagging, stared at the window; the expression on his face, coupled with the weird appearance of his completely bald head, created such a ludicrous picture that in any other circumstances, Paul would have wanted to laugh.

The silence was only of short duration, and was broken by Bob. 'Untie Mr. Rivington!' he snapped curtly. 'And don't forget I've got a gun!'

Manson relaxed his rigid attitude. 'How can I?' he snarled. 'You've broken my wrist!'

'You've got *two* hands, haven't you?'

said Bob. 'Use the other, and look sharp.'

The man hesitated; and then, apparently realising that it was useless to argue, he came over to Paul and with his uninjured hand set him free.

Paul scrambled to his feet, still dizzy from the blow he had received, but quite capable of handling the situation. Dipping his hands into Manson's overcoat pockets, he took out his own automatic and the one the man had been holding when he had first seen him.

'All right, old chap,' he said to Bob, and his brother pocketed his own weapon, and pushing up the sash climbed into the room.

'Another second and I'd have been too late,' he remarked.

'I think you would,' agreed his brother. 'Lucky for Coyne you arrived when you did.' He spoke without taking his eyes off the man he was covering. 'Take off that handkerchief,' he ordered. 'Let's have a look at you.'

The man's hand went up to his face. The handkerchief slipped down, to hang loosely round his neck. He was a stranger to Paul, but not to Bob.

'You remember my telling you about the man who was so concerned at the disappearance of Miss Fielding?' said the young man.

Paul's face was incredulous as he nodded.

'Well, there he is!' Bob jerked his head towards the man whom Coyne had addressed as Manson. 'John Royden!'

Royden must have known that his doom was sealed, but his face was expressionless. 'How did you get away?' he muttered.

'I got away,' said Bob cheerfully, 'because you didn't tie me up as securely as you thought. It took me a long time, I'll admit, to get free, but I succeeded; and once I realised where I was, I knew who'd been responsible for attacking me on the common. You saw me pick up that button, I suppose, from the window of your bedroom, guessed what I'd found, and were afraid that it would identify you as the killer of Weepers.'

'Yes,' said Royden. 'I knew I'd lost a button when I got home that night. It'd been torn off my coat, and when I saw you pick something up at the place where Weepers was killed, I guessed you'd found it.'

'It was you who put through that telephone message, supposedly from the police station?' said Bob.

Royden nodded. 'I had to think of something to get you out.' He gave a short, mirthless laugh. 'Funny how things work out, isn't it? But for my attack on you, I shouldn't have known that this was the man I'd been looking for — that this was James C. Kilroe of Johannesburg, the dirtiest blackguard who was ever born.'

'You didn't know?' said Paul.

'No!' Royden shook his head. 'How could I know? This is the first time I've ever seen him in my life.' He shrugged his shoulders. 'Well, I'm only sorry you didn't arrive a second or two later. At least he'd have got what he deserves.' His voice changed. 'By the way, I was right about Diana. He and that brute there — ' He nodded towards the dead body of Gunter. ' — were responsible for her disappearance. I got it all out of him before you arrived.' He looked at Paul. 'She knew his real name was Kilroe, and although he didn't know I was living almost next door to him any more than I did, he was scared to death that I should find him.

'That night, the night she disappeared, he went along to her room about something — part of that rheumatism gag's genuine, but it's exaggerated, for he can walk a little when he wants to — she told him about me, and that she'd promised to marry me.

'He didn't know that I was the man he was afraid of, but he was scared all the same; scared that she might let slip that his name was Kilroe, and that it would indirectly give away his whereabouts to the man he knew was looking for him. He and Gunter drugged her, and all the while you were searching the house trying to find her, she was hidden, locked in a trunk in Kilroe's bedroom.

'Gunter faked the footprints and the car and the unknown man, and packed and hid her suitcase. They'd barcly finished that piece of devilry and gone back to bed when Weepers put in an appearance. They took Diana away the following morning, after you'd gone up to town.'

'Where is she now?' asked Paul.

'Number seventeen Manette Street, Kennington,' said Royden, 'with Gunter's mother. I made him tell me that.' He looked at Bob steadily. 'I was serious about her,' he said. 'If everything had gone all right, I'd have married her, although I'd no idea she had any connection with the man I was after — the man who double-crossed my father and sent him to the Breakwater.'

'Your father was Charles Manson?' asked Paul.

'Yes.' Royden's face hardened. 'He escaped from the Breakwater and was killed when they tried to take him. He'd never have gone to the Breakwater at all if it hadn't been for him. My father and he were detectives in the employ of the Kohinoor Diamond Syndicate. I expect you know it's a criminal offence in Jo'burg to buy uncut diamonds, although there's a big profit to be made if you can do so without discovery. It was Kilroe's idea. The position he occupied gave him an advantage. He suggested the scheme to my father and he fell for it.

'They acquired an enormous quantity of stones, hundreds of thousands of pounds' worth, which cost them next to nothing. The trouble was, of course, that they couldn't dispose of them. Kilroe, however, arranged a safe hiding place, the intention being to collect them when they retired. Unfortunately for my father, the company got suspicious of the two of them; and Kilroe, getting wind of this, framed my father, and he was arrested and sent to the Breakwater.

'It wasn't until afterwards that he knew Kilroe had given him away, and he kept his mouth shut about his friend. Kilroe had two reasons for double-crossing him. One was to save his own skin, the other because with my father out of the way, the whole of the diamonds would come into his possession. His plan didn't work out quite as well as he expected, however. Although he escaped arrest, he didn't escape suspicion.

'He became aware that the company was having him watched, and decided to clear out of Jo'burg, returning after a period to collect the diamonds. He couldn't take them with him because he knew that he and all his belongings would be searched before he left the country. For this reason, also, he couldn't carry anything that showed where the diamonds were hidden, although some sort of record had to be made, otherwise he'd never be able to find the place again by himself.

'He was aware that people suspected of illicit diamond buying in South Africa are subjected to the most rigid search, even being stripped to the skin. And then the idea occurred to him to have the clue to the hiding place tattooed on his head. He resigned from the Kohinoor Company, found a man who could do what he wanted, and spent three weeks in bed until his hair grew again. Then he left for England.

'That was nearly two years ago. His intention was to go back after sufficient time had elapsed to allow himself to be forgotten by the authorities, and pick up the diamonds he'd hidden. That's Kilroe!'

'How do you come into all this?' asked Paul, as he paused.

Royden gave a short laugh. 'My father told me the whole story while he was on the Breakwater.'

'You mean you were on the Breakwater, too?'

'Yes. I was in the conspiracy, and was arrested with my father. Although, as I said, I never saw Kilroe till tonight, the three of us worked the job. I was the man he was afraid of. When he read in the paper that my father had been killed after attempting to escape, he knew he had more cause to fear than ever. I was released six months ago. He knew the date of my release, and guessed that he was in danger from that moment.'

'It's lies! Lies!' said Kilroe hoarsely. 'He's telling you a trumped-up yarn, Mr. Rivington — '

'It's the truth!' snapped Royden. 'And you know it! After my release from the Breakwater, I made enquiries about you. I'd served my sentence and I wanted my share of the stones, and my father's share. Only a third share was due to you. I had no idea of the hiding place, and I found you'd cleared out and gone to England. I managed, however, to discover you'd been to a tattooist. I found the man who told me he had tattooed a design on your head, which he'd taken from a piece of paper you gave him, and afterwards destroyed. It was part of the coastline, but he wouldn't remember which part. That, and the fact that your name was Kilroe, was the sole clue I had. I came to England three months ago.'

'You said you'd been in your present house for over two years,' put in Bob.

'I know I did.' Royden smiled. 'It was a stupid thing to do, because you could have easily found out it was a lie. But I thought, in case there was ever any suspicion against me, that would prove how impossible it could be for me to have any connection with John Manson.'

'The other two men you killed,' said Paul, 'that was a mistake?'

'Yes, it was a mistake,' admitted Royden. 'But a natural mistake. Don't forget I'd never seen Kilroe, but the name was uncommon. I could only find two, and the initials were the same. Don't forget, also, that I had to work against time. I never knew when Kilroe would return to collect the diamonds and escape me for good.'

'Why,' said Paul, 'did you kill Weepers?'

'Because he recognised me,' said Royden. 'Weepers was out in Johannesburg. We used him now and again. He knew us. I was coming home late and I saw him hanging about. He asked me for a match, and as he struck it to light his cigarette, he recognised me. I *had* to kill him. Life's funny, isn't it? Here was I searching all over the country for James Kilroe, and without knowing it, he was living opposite me all the time.'

He laughed, a quick, jerky laugh; and then, before Paul knew what he was doing or had any inkling of his intention, he suddenly lurched forward, gripped the automatic in the detective's hand by the barrel, pressed it against his breast, and jerked Paul's trigger-finger.

There was an explosion. Royden gave a

convulsive start, and sank to the floor.

When Paul and Bob bent over him, he was dead.

26

Aftermath

'I saved the country the cost of a trial,' said Paul wearily as he leant back in the uncomfortable chair in Mr. Robin's cheerless office. 'And lost the hangman a fee.'

'Well, I'm glad it's all cleared up, anyway,' the inspector said. 'The assistant commissioner was beginning to get a bit unpleasant. Did you find Miss Fielding all right?'

Paul nodded. 'Yes; she's been taken to hospital. They kept her under the influence of dope, and when we discovered her, she was so dazed she couldn't speak coherently. The woman who was looking after her, Gunter's mother, is in Kennington police station.'

'Best place for her,' said the inspector. 'You've made it all clear except one thing. If this fellow Royden, or Manson, had no idea Coyne was the Kilroe he was looking for, why did he make those attempts on his life?'

'He didn't.'

'Then who did?'

'Nobody. Those were purely figments of Coyne's invention. He knew that the son of the man he had double-crossed and sent to the Breakwater had been released, and knew he was looking for him. He wanted protection, and because of his own position he couldn't go to the police. So with Gunter, whom he had got hold of and taken into his confidence, he hatched a scheme for getting me down.

'He sent Diana Fielding — who, by the way, isn't the child of a dead friend at all, but his step-daughter — to bring me down, and told me this rigmarole of three attempts on his life and his fear of a fourth. In order to make the thing look convincing, and to impress me still further, he arranged with Diana to send that wire, his idea being that if the man who was looking for him knew I was in the house, it'd scare him off.'

'I see.' Mr. Robin frowned and fiddled

with a pen-holder. 'What was the idea of passing her off as his ward if she was his step-daughter?'

'Simply to make it more difficult for anyone to identify him. He's yellow all through. One of the most unpleasant characters I've met.'

'Well, nobody will have a chance of meeting him for some years to come,' said the Scotland Yard man. 'He'll get a heavy sentence if this diamond business can be proved against him.'

'And he deserves it,' said Rivington curtly.

'What's going to happen to Miss Fielding?' asked the inspector after a pause. 'If she really was in love with this fellow Royden, it's going to be a shock to her when she finds out.'

Paul nodded gravely. 'I think the whole thing will be a shock to her. Though I doubt very much if she can have a worse time in store than she's had living with Coyne. I'm going to see what I can do in the way of getting her some sort of job.'

'What was all this stuff you told me about a fourth Mr. Kilroe?' asked Round

Robin. 'I've heard of three, but what did you mean about the other?'

'I was going to be the other.' Paul smiled. 'I thought I might draw out our murderer. As it turned out, it wasn't necessary.'

'I see. Bait, eh?'

'Exactly.' Paul yawned and rose to his feet. 'Well, I think I'll be getting home. I'm still feeling a little out of sorts from that bang on the head.'

'Go and have a good sleep,' said Round Robin. 'That'll do you more good than anything.'

'I think you're right,' said Paul; and he took his leave, to adopt the advice his friend had offered.

GRIM DEATH
MURDER IN MANUSCRIPT
THE GLASS ARROW
THE THIRD KEY
THE ROYAL FLUSH MURDERS
THE SQUEALER
MR. WHIPPLE EXPLAINS
THE SEVEN CLUES
THE CHAINED MAN
THE HOUSE OF THE GOAT
THE FOOTBALL POOL MURDERS
THE HAND OF FEAR
SORCERER'S HOUSE
THE HANGMAN
THE CON MAN
MISTER BIG
THE JOCKEY
THE SILVER HORSESHOE
THE TUDOR GARDEN MYSTERY
THE SHOW MUST GO ON
SINISTER HOUSE
THE WITCHES' MOON
ALIAS THE GHOST
THE LADY OF DOOM
THE BLACK HUNCHBACK

PHANTOM HOLLOW
WHITE WIG
THE GHOST SQUAD
THE NEXT TO DIE
THE WHISPERING WOMAN
THE TWELVE APOSTLES
THE GRIM JOKER
THE HUNTSMAN
THE NIGHTMARE MURDERS
THE TIPSTER
THE VAMPIRE MAN
THE RED TAPE MURDERS

with Chris Verner:
THE BIG FELLOW
THE SNARK WAS A BOOJUM

We do hope that you have enjoyed reading this large print book.

Did you know that all of our titles are available for purchase?

We publish a wide range of high quality large print books including:
Romances, Mysteries, Classics
General Fiction
Non Fiction and Westerns

Special interest titles available in large print are:
The Little Oxford Dictionary
Music Book, Song Book
Hymn Book, Service Book

Also available from us courtesy of Oxford University Press:
Young Readers' Dictionary
(large print edition)
Young Readers' Thesaurus
(large print edition)

For further information or a free brochure, please contact us at:
Ulverscroft Large Print Books Ltd.,
The Green, Bradgate Road, Anstey,
Leicester, LE7 7FU, England.
Tel: (00 44) **0116 236 4325**
Fax: (00 44) **0116 234 0205**

COLD CALLING

Geraldine Ryan

Pronounced unfit for frontline duty due to injury, and eligible to retire in a year, DS Fran Phoenix is given a new job heading up the cold cases team — or 'put in a corner' in the basement, as she sees it. Teamed up with a PC with barely two years' experience, they reopen the twenty-five-year-old case of a missing girl — but evidence continues to be thin on the ground. Can the oddly matched duo heat up the trail and uncover the truth? Three stories from the pen of Geraldine Ryan.

LORD JAMES HARRINGTON AND THE CORNISH MYSTERY

Lynn Florkiewicz

While on holiday with his wife Beth in Cornwall, James learns that a local fisherman vanished during the recent opening procession of the Cornish Legends Festival. When more men disappear in broad daylight, he can't help but put his sleuthing hat on. If they were kidnapped, why is there no ransom demand? What are the flashing lights off the coastline? Who is the eccentric woman on the moors? Have the Cornish Legends really come to life? As James delves into the mystery, he realizes his questions come at a price . . .